BAD WORDS

THE
SEAGULL
LIBRARY OF
GERMAN
LITERATURE

Bad Words

Selected Short Prose

ILSE AICHINGER

TRANSLATED BY ULJANA WOLF
AND CHRISTIAN HAWKEY

LONDON NEW YORK CALCUTTA

This publication was supported by a grant from
the Goethe-Institut, India.

The original English translation of this title was supported by a grant
from the Austrian Federal Ministry for Education, Arts and Culture.

Seagull Books, 2022

ISBN   978 1 8030 9 046 7

British Library Cataloguing-in-Publication Data
A catalogue record for this book is available from the British Library

Typeset by Seagull Books, Calcutta, India
Printed and bound by WordsWorth India, New Delhi, India

CONTENTS

A Werldly Country

On Ilse Aichinger and Her Language

When Hans Werner Richter—initiator of the Gruppe 47 meetings which helped shape much of Germany's postwar literature—visited the young writer Ilse Aichinger in Vienna in 1952 to invite her for the next meeting in Niendorf at the Baltic Sea, another younger woman was sitting shyly on the sofa. Her name was Ingeborg Bachmann, and Richter had never heard of her. After reading her poems a few days later, he promptly invited her, and—upon her request—extended the invitation to another rather unknown poet, 'a friend of hers from Paris'. Thus, not only Ilse Aichinger but also Ingeborg Bachmann and Paul Celan took part in the group's next meeting, which—even though Celan's reading of 'Todesfuge' was, according to its members, famously ill-conceived—stood for a paradigm shift away from neorealist to more complex forms of literature. Yet while Bachmann and Celan have through numerous translations become known as two of the most important writers of postwar German poetry, Aichinger has remained somewhat overlooked in the English- speaking world.

Born in 1921, Ilse Aichinger survived the Second World War with her Jewish mother in Vienna. According to the Nuremberg Laws, her mother was protected as long as she lived in the same household with her minor daughter—a 'first-degree half-breed'. Many of their relatives, including Aichinger's beloved grandmother, were deported in 1942 and died in concentration camps. Aichinger's twin sister Helga managed to escape with one of the last *Kindertransporte* to England—a place that since then has taken on mythical dimensions in Aichinger's poetic topography and in the prose poems published here. In 1945, Aichinger published the piece 'Das vierte Tor' (The Fourth Gate) about the Jewish cemetery in Vienna; this text was the first to mention the Holocaust in Austrian literature. In 1948, the year that saw the appearance of Celan's *Der Sand aus den Urnen* (The Sand from the Urns) and the disappearing of Orson Welles' 'Third Man' in Vienna's underground water tunnels, Aichinger's first and only novel *Die größere Hoffnung* (*The Greater Hope*) was published in Amsterdam. Portraying the life of Jewish and persecuted children in Nazi Vienna, the novel established Ilse Aichinger as a major figure in postwar writing; the literary critic Richard Reichensperger noted that 'Ilse Aichinger is the beginning of postwar

Austrian literature.' Thanks to a new translation by the Austrian translator and literary scholar Geoff Wilkes, this profound poetic meditation on exclusion, survival and the transcendence of those experiences, is now readily available to a larger audience—marking, one shall hope, the beginning of an international recognition of Aichinger that is long overdue.[1]

Back to the 1952 meeting: At the end of the readings, Aichinger was awarded the prize of the Gruppe 47 for her *Spiegelgeschichte* (Story in a Mirror). The story narrates the life of a female protagonist from death onward, that is, in reverse, which earned Aichinger the problematic nickname 'Fräulein Kafka'. In an earlier piece, Aichinger had proclaimed that the only possible narration was 'from the end and towards the end'; the experience of fear, death and destruction of the Shoah became the starting point for a new narration, a new kind of writing.

1 See Ilse Aichinger, *The Greater Hope* (Geoff Wilkes trans.) (Würz-burg: Königshausen and Neumann, 2016). Other recent publications include: Gail Wiltshire's monogram, *A Spatial Reading of Ilse Aichinger's Novel* Die größere Hoffnung (Würzburg: Königshausen and Neumann, 2015); and the reprint of Eric Mosbacher's 1955 translation of one of Aichinger's early short story collections, *The Bound Man, and Other Stories* (London: Copy Press, 2015).

One year earlier, in his acceptance speech for the Bremer Literature Prize, Paul Celan had said:

> It, the language, remained, not lost, yes, in spite of everything. But it had to pass through its own answerlessness, pass through frightful muting, pass through the thousand darknesses of deathbringing speech. It passed through and gave back no words for that which happened; yet it passed through this happening. Passed through and could come to light again, 'enriched' by all this.[2]

Both Celan and Aichinger experienced this process of 'Sprachwerdung' as a strong and irreversible estrangement and foreignization of and in their languages. At the end of the 1960s, after writing a novel, poems and short stories, Aichinger started to work on short prose pieces that can only be described as long prose poems marked by a radical poetics of opacity and an unassuming, often startling beauty. The prelude to this most interesting part of her work is *My Language and I* (1967), beginning with the words: 'My language is one that tends towards foreign words. I choose them, I

2 Paul Celan, *Selected Poems and Prose* (John Felstiner trans.) (New York and London: W.W. Norton, 2001), p. 395.

retrieve them from far away. But it is a small language. It doesn't reach far. All around, all around me, always all around and so forth. We advance against our will. To hell with us, I sometimes say to it.' The story that follows describes an absurd picnic with 'my language' as a real presence that refuses to talk to the narrator, constantly loses things, and—very Gertrude Stein—prefers cold food rather than warm.

Surprisingly though, the words used here are not very foreign. Foreignness, rather, seems to be a fundamental relation between self and language that enables another kind of speaking, one that bears witness to the 'silencing' without falling into silence itself, and which instead functions as a constant documentation of the falling, and the failing: 'Writing is learning to die', Aichinger noted in her collection *Kleist, Moos, Fasane* (1987). To get the attention of her estranged and seemingly disinterested language, the narrator takes up a knife and lets it fall from a high distance onto a plate. Foreignness here is also a place or site— a picnic that takes place near the border-crossing station of another country. 'The fourth country has ended, I shouted in its ear, the fifth is already over there', is how the narrator tries to choose a spot for the picnic. Yet the agents of domestication, in this case 'Customs officers', loom in the background.

In pushing these literal and literary boundaries, Aichinger's writing takes up civic responsibility by refusing to accept old notions—notions advanced by nineteenth-century European formulations of the nation-state and the subsequent unfolding of its ongoing disasters—of the self and the body, or of language, power, borders and belonging. 'I have only one language, and it's not mine. . . . Language is something that doesn't belong'—in *Monolingualism of the Other* (1998), Jacques Derrida reflects on his origins as a French Jew in Algeria as marked by a threefold linguistic and geopolitical experience of distance, borders and bans imposed by the dominating but far-off mother country France and the Vichy regime. In contrast, Aichinger's monolingualism—her one language —is 'of the other' because it is destabilized from the inside, forever foreignized by the memory of the time when language 'gave back no words for that which happened'—memory kept alive by distrusting and deconstructing notions of logic, cohesion and coherence.

These poetics of opacity and resistance culminate in the 1976 prose poem collection *Schlechte Wörter* (Bad

Words)—which is presented here for the first time in English in its entirety, together with short stories from the preceding collection *Eliza, Eliza* (1968)—making accessible the full arc of Aichinger's most experimental middle-period work. In the title story, the narrator proclaims: 'I now no longer use better words.' All systems of meaning and referentiality are rejected: 'No one can demand that I make connections as long as they're avoidable.' What we normally think of as reality is disposed of in these prose poems or, rather, taken apart and left to consider in a language that uses only the 'second-best words', as the first story of the collection proclaims. The style of these texts is matter-of-fact, yet they offer neither facts nor matters in ways we're used to. Doubt is the only certainty and the focus is always on minor things or second-best objects —stains, balconies, apple rice. The protagonists of those pieces—the drooling ones, the lost ones, the weak ones, 'prompters and opera-glass manufacturers'—are Beckett's heroes, turned Austrian.

This refusal of imposed correspondences, or connections, including those imposed by the constraints of language, has some relation to Modernist experimentation and Postmodernist notions of linguistic indeterminacy. Yet with Aichinger one senses a rejection of

Enlightenment-era systems of classification and ordering, including the classification of indeterminacy, as well as an effort to dramatize that effort, make it sensible. With Stein or Beckett their resistances are often wilfully celebratory; with Aichinger there is a sense that the stakes are too high to celebrate. It's not fear but a kind of vigilant caution which brings her work, in this regard, closer to Kafka's.

Aichinger's effort to insist on entangled relation, to dramatize a radical contingency between herself and the reader, as well as her wish to leave behind false promises about the coherence of the world and its 'better words', lead to a language deploying only 'bad words'—bad because they have been stripped off their misleading certainties, opinions and ideologies. It is through the deployment of 'inexact' words that Aichinger enables her language to survive and re-invent itself: 'Werld would be better than world. Less useful, less skilful.' Language, foreignized by its will to be radically inadequate—only to reclaim it adequately for the purposes of poetry. 'I don't control anything,' says the narrator in 'The Mouse', 'I am only being present.'

Translating Ilse Aichinger is challenging precisely because of this linguistic presence which manifests itself as the impossibility of establishing adequate interpretations or stable external explanations. 'Den Augenblick aufrechterhalten', *to keep alive the moment*, reads a sparse note from a 1960 journal. On a stylistic level, Aichinger's many grammatical and syntactical idiosyncrasies can be read as an expression of this prolonged being-present in a language that does not belong: The use of proper names (of mostly identifiable places, like 'Dover', and mostly unidentifiable people or things, like 'Hemlin' or 'Jenkins'); the excessive use of pronouns as a way to heighten the self-referentiality of language ('*This can't be it*. But this is it')—even more problematic when many of the gendered pronouns in German will simply translate as 'it' in English; the foreignization of idioms and common phrases, mostly taking them literally; unprompted use of repetitions and rhetorical questions; or, finally, an intense preoccupation with the prefixes and suffixes of words which are often repeated and then slightly altered to achieve an effect of estrangement which, in an inflected language like German, effectively demonstrates and simultaneously demolishes the structural determinacy of language, and with it, the possibility of fixed meanings.

Aichinger's emphasis on the inadequate challenges the very heart of translation: How can a translation be adequate if the original refuses to be whole, exact, determinate? If the poetics of this writing insists on using 'second-best words', how to choose the 'right' ones in the target language? Ultimately, in translating Aichinger, our goal was to carry across this resistance: resist making more sense, resist filling in the gaps, resist making references more clear, resist straightening the grammar. Would such a translation always risk seeming inadequately translated? Would it always risk reading like a translation? 'The stains win. They also win.'

Of the many challenging instances in these texts, here is, by way of example, a brief discussion of the text 'Snow', which was chosen as a coda to this volume because it was written in 1975, at the same time as the other texts from *Bad Words*, though published much later, and because it stands as a poetic witness to the author's continuous (and sometimes hilarious) examination of the boundaries of expression.

In this short text, Ilse Aichinger juxtaposes the German prefix *be,* as in 'beschneit', and the prefix *ver-*, as in 'verschneit'. Both words translate as 'snow-covered'. The narrator prefers the prefix *ver-*, noting that its letters form the second part of the word Dover, a place of geopoetical importance in Aichinger's world, and a reference to the story 'Dover' from *Bad Words*.

More importantly, the prefix *ver-*, as derived from gothic *fra*, suggests to the narrator a sense of disappearing ('Verschwinden') as well as downfall or disaster ('Zugrundegehen') which seems sufficient proof that the prefix 'belong[s] to snow and snowing a thousand times more than any other prefix'. Even a source is quoted: *Die Vorsilbe ver- und ihre Geschichte, Breslau 1907* (The Prefix *ver-* and Its History), a book that actually exists and was also part of Aichinger's library.

The translation of the play on prefixes poses multiple difficulties: English does not offer a similarly important and versatile prefix as *ver-* (the English prefixes derived from the same root are per-, pre-, pro-, and for-). Of the ones that exist, none seem to work with 'snow' or 'snowed', let alone suggest a similar connotation of disappearance and disaster. But deeming this text an important example of Aichinger's dark humour despite disaster, we did not want to leave it untranslated. Instead we chose to approximate the juxtaposition of prefixes by using 'bensnowed' and 'encased in snow', and by recreating a reference to a non-existing linguistic publication about the prefix *en-*, that coincidentally makes up the first part of the word English. By failing to ferry across the right prefix and the real-life source-book reference, the translation ends up enacting, rather than mirroring, the original text: English makes *ver-* of *Verschwinden* disappear, becoming instead a sort of snow on the original. 'Snow is a word and so is hay. Snow is a word. There aren't many words.'

Uljana Wolf and Christian Hawkey
New York, Berlin, Rome
October 2016–November 2017

MY LANGUAGE AND I

I

My memory I left in a ravine,—
Casual louse that tissues the buckwheat,
Aprons rocks, congregates pears
In moonlit bushels
And wakens alleys with a hidden cough.

Hart Crane

just to leap forward to another
attacked and limited riddle

Helga Michie

My Green Donkey

Every day I see a green donkey walk over the railway bridge, hooves clattering on the planks, head visible above the railing. I don't know where he comes from, I haven't yet managed to observe this. But I suspect he comes from the shut-down electricity plant on the other side of the bridge, where the road runs like an arrow to the north-west (a direction I never knew what to do with anyhow), and where, in the crumbling entranceway, soldiers sometimes stand and put their arms around their girls as soon as it gets dark and nothing but a weak scrap of light hovers over the rusty roof. But my donkey comes earlier. Which is not to say that he comes as soon as noon, or shortly after, when the glaring sun still pierces every single one of the abandoned courtyards and through the cracks of the boarded-up windows. No, he comes with the first imperceptible weakening of light and then I see him, usually already up on the footbridge, or as he's climbing the stairs. Only once did I see him clattering over the cobblestones on the other side of the train tracks—but he looked hurried, as if he were running late. At the time it seemed to me, incidentally, that he had come directly out of the half-open, motionless, sun-baked gate of the old electricity plant.

He couldn't care less about train employees or other folks who pass along the bridge, he dodges them politely; and the stomping and whistling of trains that sometimes pass underneath while he crosses the bridge does not bother him either. Often he turns his head sideways and looks down, usually when there is no train approaching, and never for very long. It appears to me as if he were exchanging a few words with the train tracks, but that's quite impossible. And what would be the point of that? Just beyond the middle of the bridge he disappears, after some hesitation, without turning back. This—the nature of his disappearing— I'm not mistaken about. And frankly I understand it quite well: Why should he trouble himself and turn around, since he knows the way, after all?

But how does he come, from where does he come, where does he originate? Does he have a mother or a bed of hay in one of the silent courtyards? Or does he inhabit one of the former offices, does he have a corner there, something familiar, a part of a wall? Or does he

4

originate like lightning originates between the ancient high-tension poles, the dangling lines? Of course I don't exactly know how lightning originates, and I don't want to know unless my donkey originated the same way. *My* donkey? That's a big word. But I don't want to take it back. It's quite possible that others see him too—but I won't ask them. My donkey, who I don't feed and don't water, whose coat I don't comb, and who I don't comfort. But whose silhouette stands out against the far, far mountains as unmistakably as the mountains themselves stand out against the afternoon. In my eyes, therefore my donkey. Why should I not confess that I begin to live the moment he arrives? That his appearance creates the air I breathe, him especially—his silhouette, the shade of his green, the way he lowers his head to look down on the tracks? I thought that perhaps he was hungry and looking for the grass and scanty weeds that grow between the railroad ties. But one really ought to restrain one's compassion. I'm too old for that, I won't bring a bundle of hay and place it on the bridge for him. And he doesn't look bad, not starving and not tormented—also not very well. But few donkeys look well, I guess. I don't want to repeat old mistakes—I don't want to ask too much of him. I want to be content with expecting him, or rather: with not expecting him. For he doesn't come regularly. Did I mention this? Twice already he didn't come. I hesitate to write this, for who knows, perhaps this is his rhythm, perhaps in his world there is no such thing as twice and, therefore, he always came, always came regularly, and would be astonished about my lament. He seems to be astonished about many things, come to think of it.

Astonishment, yes, that's what describes him best, what distinguishes him, I guess. I want to learn to confine myself to guesswork for everything concerning him—later even to less. But until then many things still trouble me. More than his possible hunger, for example, there is the fact that I don't know the location of his sleep, of his rest, and therefore possibly of his birth. Quite certainly he needs rest. It could even be that each time he needs death. I don't know. I think it must be exhausting, to cross the bridge every evening, as green as he is, and to look down as he does, and then to disappear at the right moment.

Such a donkey needs rest, much rest. And is an old electricity plant really the right place, does it suffice? And the dangling electric lines, do they caress him softly enough during his night when he is not on the bridge? For his night is longer than ours. And the silhouettes of the mountains, do they demonstrate sufficiently their friendship during his day? For his day is shorter. As always, I don't know. And I will never find out, for my aim can only be to know less and less about him—this much I've learnt, during the six months that he's been coming. Learnt from him. And so perhaps I will also learn to endure the day when he stops coming—for this is what I'm afraid of. He might stay away with the cold, and this staying away could be a part of his coming as much as the coming itself. But until this point I want to learn to know so little about him that I will finally be able to endure his staying away, and I won't lay my eyes on the bridge any more.

But until this moment, I sometimes dream that he might have a green father and a green mother, and a bundle of hay in one of the courtyards, and in his ears the laughter of young people squeezing into the entranceway. And that he sometimes sleeps, instead of dying.

My Father Made from Straw

My father lives in the old shed, my father holds out on the ice. Anyone who doesn't believe this can come with me and visit him, they can slip through the reeds and in the winter through the tar, and they will see him instantly, he's not far away—we don't care much for distance these days. My father sits in the old armchair and he is made entirely from straw. He warms his left hand on a piece of wall, his right hand on a piece of iron that still stands there. My father sailed with Amundsen, he knows the Lower Seas. He wears his uniform, it's old—he is an old railroader and old railroaders are industrious, they've always divided up the bales of hay fairly. They used to walk up and down between the rails, and you could hear their shouts against the snow, and often someone who lived far away placed his hand on his grandson's hat and said: Do you hear? Do you hear them? Back then they kept the swarms of crows off the rails, no one knows what that means. Swarms of crows?, they say now, laughing. They laugh way too much. Back then people used to have models made from straw, and everything was first tried out with straw: rail construction, rail system, signals. Now we're far beyond that, we've moved on, there are no crows, no straw, but my father doesn't care, he holds out in the couch house, he holds out on the ice. He won't let go of the world. He lifts his straw hand and looks through the broken window, into white air. Next to the piece of iron there's a box with wood, sometimes he bends down and rummages around in it. The old railroaders were familiar with everything, they knew all the mills and all the owls along the track, they knew them well. Not like today, when someone casually says: The owls' nests are to the left. Back then they didn't approve of such things. Left or right didn't matter, but the distance between the rails, and in between the bumps and hollows in the ground, and the tension lines taut or untaut, and the small barrels frozen in puddles of rainwater—everything had to be exact. Surely they already had their ways back then but is this the reason? Everything was measured in straw, in single and doubled rail widths. And people gladly delivered the straw, they brought it down to the shed in sacks, often a long way through the rain. Straw, that was the thing back then, and my father is still made from straw today. He has no choice, but he doesn't want to be made of anything else. Wax lost its appeal to him long ago. Perhaps it appealed to him earlier when he was a child and saw beehives, and saw how they built their artful combs—but he's over that, he doesn't want to trade places with anyone. He doesn't envy anyone. Sometimes the boilerman comes and walks into his office, throwing himself on the bed, and begins to moan. One time he got up and came out and in his dream he tried to quarrel with my father, but nothing doing, my father didn't want to have anything to do with him. You always end up misinterpreted when you get involved with people who are dreaming. And he is just an average boilerman, not too strongly built. But he came rushing out of the room, arms thrown up, and he shook my father till the straw flew left and right. This also used to be different. Not that all the old railroaders had the same dream, but no matter how many dreams there were—a fight was always possible. Often one would hear their voices far away, the same monosyllabic shouts as when they were at work; the grandchildren trembled but no one else seemed upset.

Sometimes a miller from the old folks' home comes to visit my father, still wearing his white hat and his white suit, and often you don't notice him for a long time when he comes through the snow. He will talk about his Christmas celebration and his glass terrace, and my father listens eagerly, his head bent down. The miller always puts plants and ferns in the glass terrace during the holiday season—they attract light, sparks, like with the old trains. My father is pleased when the old miller visits, but the miller is not his only visitor. Donkeys, cows, and small wild animals often hop over the rails to brush against his old uniform, shivering, sniffing. Also animals with horns or stripes, hyenas even, and gazelles, and always behind them the shepherds. This is a tableau. The shepherds wail and shout and shoo the animals out of the shed. One time one of them accidently brushed off my father's hat in the heat, but my father didn't mind, from the old railroad my father is used to all kinds of things. And the shepherd picked up the hat again, and that was that. And if it weren't for the shepherds' shouting, my father would prefer the animals over the miller. The miller is too big, he almost pushes my father off the chair every time he visits, and he rarely sits down at his feet.

The others often mock me and say I have a straw man for a father. With a straw hat, they shout, knowing how wrong they are, with a suit made of straw, their voices shrieking, and with buttons made of straw! Even buttonholes made of straw, a rude person once

11

shouted, as if there was such a thing: holes made of straw. But they only shout because they envy me. Because none of them has a father who sits in a shed day in, day out, and only now and then bends his head and snaps his fingers, or rummages around in the wood. Because none of their fathers would be content with a view of bright ice through a single small broken window. Their fathers need excavation services and long nights, but my father doesn't need any of that. He's made of straw, that's true, but the old railroaders are all made of straw, and the millers along the tracks can tell you a thing or two about that. Straw burns easily, and one of them once caught fire, jumped off the train and ran through the thistles, burning. He illuminated the river, and the ice chunks in the river, no one would dare do that today. No one is made of straw, and if he were, he wouldn't admit it, especially folks from the railroad, they think it's too dangerous now. And yet heads made of straw are beautiful, the air filters easily through them, even the heavy air in the shed; my father has many thoughts. He thinks about the ice when it freezes, the slipperiness of windowpanes when it melts, the humidity when his limbs hurt. About the shepherds, the animals, the miller, everything. No one thinks as much as he does. The miller is made of flesh and bone, but the miller doesn't think. And the shepherds? Who would expect them to think? Once there was a little hyena with thoughts in her head, and she was inseparable from my father. But people didn't notice, and later the hyena drowned by the lumber mill, in the very same pond where the logs and boards float. I'm not saying it's malice, but nowadays people don't know much about anything any more. They gather in groups, they march up and down the hills with music and wreaths, but they don't know anything about my father, that's beyond them. Where would we be, they say, if we had to also bother with the straw? Never mind that the straw wears hats and wears pants, it's still only straw. That's the way they talk, these are the words you hear if you find yourself standing in a hallway next to them as they return from work and don't see you. In my ears, this is blasphemy, and I pray when I hear it. Then I quickly give them back the freshly sharpened sickles, or whatever it is that such people need, running back and forth like they do, or carved into brightly lit rooms like pieces of wood—and again I retreat to the shed. I slip under their electric lines, I slide down their slippery, sterile pastures, and I hear their horses whinny behind me, but I'm already gone. Happiness chases me over the river stones to my father made of straw. Clouds pass above, or planets or the mild air, but I know where I'm going, and nothing else can delight me now.

There are some who say I run so fast because I fear for my father. But I don't fear the millers and the boilermen, or the shepherds and their animals either. It's true, shepherds deal with fire, everyone knows this, that's where we get our campfires. And a boilerman— no need to explain. And same with the gazelles and the other animals, that would be called a bushfire. But still I am relieved when the sky is grey and glazed over, and when no redness of dusk or dawn sparks fear and discontent in my heart. Because I can't protect my father—not from the senseless and ambitious cheerfulness of others, and not from his own wishes. I fear the stars, because the truth is that my father wants to journey to the stars. But what is that, a journey to the stars, how am I supposed to understand? My father doesn't explain. Does he mean softness, enclosed pastures, reeds and old age? I don't know. I only notice that he raises his head with a jolt when a star passes by his slanted, icy window, that he stops rummaging around in his box of wood. And indeed, so far above they resemble nothing more than distant bundles of straw, burning and spinning. But I can't ask my father if he considers them his companions, and I don't even wish that I could. I only want him to stay for a little while longer, here in his old armchair in the shed, quiet and damp as he is, even with the musty smell that often sticks to things like old uniforms and straw.

Did I forget to mention how my father is drawn to icicles? He likes them better than all the wood in his box, and I bring him some as often as I can. I break them off from barn roofs, at random, I take them as they come, and the dogs are after me. There he is again, the icicle-breaker! I hear them shout from afar, to no avail. When my father is surrounded by the icicles, in circles and half circles, bright as the shafts of spears, but smarter, he is most content. He no longer tosses his head towards the stars, and the angels shine on him.

The Mouse

I bump into everything, but I don't like to bump heads. I'm informed about traps. But this here is not a trap, there is a pleasant reddish light and it is mild. I hear steps everywhere: human steps, duck steps, the steps of dream walkers, sons and daughters, there are many, the steps of the righteous, I can easily tell them apart. Every now and then a brighter light seeps through the cracks, which makes me think I could get out of here, but I rein in this thought, I don't entertain it. I entertain fear, that's better—it asks of me nothing other than myself. I weigh it and let it come over me, from one side to the other, thus I learn to distinguish directions. There is not much space here, but there are directions and they have no limit. They too are mild and they don't come over me. When I move my ears I brush the wood, it is rough and I like smelling it. But fear is better, it is rewarding and I imagine it as a large white blossom swaying in the morning wind (surely on a stem); fearful people don't pick it. But the neighbour's children whoop and holler at it and its smell fills my nostrils. I'm being put in my place, this much I know, and you can't miss it, once you're placed there. And you are. I feel just like the people who gather in arbours in the evening, but I don't know why—I don't go into the house like they do, and a web of shadows covers me. I don't go into the house because I can't, but why always point out what separates us? And why can't I go in? Because of the closed doors and the larger animals lingering around the house—those and other external reasons? Or is it because I can't get out of here? But who knows whether they can? Or whether I can't? Let's forget about the people in the arbour, I shouldn't have mentioned them. The neighbour's children are better—with their horses (it's true, one of them has a horse, though he lives far away and that's pretty much all he has), or the dog up in the tree. They found it after it had been hanging there for a long time—they talked about it loudly. Or the mushroom pickers whose voices and steps I often hear, though it doesn't make me happy. And the pilgrims, all those people! Almost everything leads us too far. So let's stay in this place, right where I am, as the song goes. Not a song that's otherwise easily accessible for the likes of us. Which is why this place seems suspicious to me. Because it is a trap, perhaps? Because it is not a trap? This is what I ask myself. I don't need any-one's pity. No one should rush, or even slam a screen door a bit more sharply because of me. That would be embarrassing. No one should come for me with wires and iron and try to save me, it would only cause a dis-turbance, and the voices and smells outside would pass unheard. Which would be a shame, even when it comes to the voices of the mushroom pickers. The mushroom pickers rarely listen to each other, and so their words would rise over the woods, into the air, into those old, miserable hideaways, all the words and syllables and even smaller things, forever alone and untraceable. Because there they easily and never go together, easily and never, this is the reason—and I don't want this to happen to them, not to the words, not to the syllables and to whatever else they become —clumps, rumours—and not even to the air which abandons me. And so I'm here and I listen, my ears are sharp, and when they brush the wood they also brush the neighbouring fields of ice—I don't control any-thing, I am merely being present. This is one advantage of my situation. Everyone else can easily be suspected of wanting to control, usurp, rule over something. But not me. I hear the ice break with as much interest as disinterest, I will keep this balance as long as I'm here.

And I don't privilege one thing over the other, neither stomping grounds, nor streams surrounded by lofty mountains, nor dreamers—I am equally good to all of them. Something that gives way underfoot is just as important as bunkers with double or triple false bottoms that need to be blown up in the end. I don't bear grudges, I can tame my preferences—but I can only do it here. Once outside, who knows if I wouldn't begin to judge the frozen lions, or start to sniff at bridges, define values, or simply take measurements—which is suspicious in itself. The smell of the wood would attract me, scuff marks, old lights, the bellowing of deer. But not here. The measurements of this place are so small they can hardly be called measurements—they are above suspicion. This is not a house and not a stable, not a pleasant or unpleasant surprise, no need for bunches of laurel or carnations on the fence. No furs, no feathers of crows on the wall outside, not even one nail. I like it this way. No bird must bite the dust because of me, no flood must surge, no sunrise for me, this is good. All laughter happens without me. But what if I attempted to get out of here, if I made one single step, in one direction? Everything would change. No matter if I found an exit, or found that there is no exit—nothing would be the same as before. Exit or no exit, it would mean the same thing once I knew it. I could not rejoice any more, my heart would be silent—a miserable thing, a far-fetched guess, even on the freest hill. No, someone in my situation should never let exits come too close, should never consider them, or approach them even with the slightest movement. Not one floorboard shall lift, no warmth slip in from the outside, nothing sweet shall harm me, no breeze. Only then will the web of shadows on my back change and forever become my markings, and my situation will become my form. But what about the paralysis which I can't seem to escape, the dank cold that encapsulates me? One should never spell out every hope. One should be like the bridges which leave, even after they collapse, every step to people who merely touch them, who jump back at first sight, who never step on them—I know a few of those people. It's hard to believe how many collapsed bridges exist, but still there are numerous methods to cross the ice—circles, detours, U-turns, turns through thickets, through snow, past timber yards, no lack. A garden of frost flowers, even random things found at its edges— mittens, handkerchiefs, kindly speared on sticks. All you mushroom pickers and snow lights, all my friends: Look this far, but not further. Set your sights on what's in sight. Go further, go further, don't mind the moon chimes, just don't rush to me. And you too, neighbour's children, go ahead, lift up the blossoms and grow. Deny your own boldness, don't free me! Because I don't want a mirror, or a pane of glass, not even a murky handful of water to reflect my image back to me. Who knows, perhaps I rejoice because I am untraceable.

The Arrival

They suggested taking a walk through the vineyards, but I declined. It was already dark, I reckoned. But darkness, they replied, was the best time to observe the white oxen hauling home their last loads (they seem, at this hour, to have risen directly out of ancient myths), and to smell the wood of the barrels, to see the whitish low walls shimmer in the dusk between rows of vines, the steeples of neighbouring villages, towns. What pretence are you using this time?, my brother asked. To be tense, I said, because indeed there are pretexts that match, or mask, you can't take them seriously enough. He laughed and went downstairs, and I heard his steps creak on the staircase, I listened intently to this creaking, it was better than an answer, better than white oxen, not risen from ancient myths. Then I heard the voice of his wife, the voice of his hireling (for they do have a hireling here, and they are proud of him, and surely I understand: a hireling, our hireling; perhaps only *one* hireling, Giuliano or something—no bed of roses in the wretched garden in front of the wretched house, no incense in the hallway that divides kitchen and parlour, but a hireling, Giuliano), and the laughter of his children, a lingering storm of laughter. Wasn't it true that one sense alone makes a house more palpable—more so than two, three or seven senses, especially in unfamiliar places?

I leant against the wall and looked closely at the room I'd been given, the black window frames and the candle in the iron holder on the night stand, an unlit room, a silent room, not much youth, not much age, I cherished it. I grasped its humble and austere accessibility, the smell of seemliness which encloses all other smells—how long did I grasp it? Wasn't this a room to let one's suitcase stand next to the wall, unopened, perhaps for ever? I tried to remember the moment I had entered it, for it is better to remember things while they are happening, or shortly afterwards. I didn't have to close my eyes: the walls above the bed and the yellow pillows possessed plenty of the light which is best taken in by closed eyes; it was easy to remember. Only the miserable trees on both sides of the street on the way from the train station intervened with their crackling. Whose memory could ever do without these trees, without the wooden, teetering constructions inside his dreams? I bent down and moved the suit-cases to the window.

Everything still lay ahead of me. The long dinners and the short dinners, the glasses of wine, the rides to church in my brother's rickety car, the giggling and chattering children, many hours of it. And I could sum them all up in one night, in one gaze at the white but sombre walls, or in a few quick steps from dresser to bed. I could embrace, with the four bedposts, everyone I was going to meet here, and they would never know. And I could observe in the changing shadows outside the window the images of the saints I might need for protection in this house. And with the night air streaming in I could greet the lukewarm, desperate, sun-perforated wind with which the excursions to the ruins and the more distant lakes would soon begin, and with which we would return home. How disturbing to call this home, this unknown place, and to have har-vested the fruit for many years, and to keep harvesting it, with children and grandchildren, with ladders and with baskets. How strange to be driving to church here on Sundays, and home again, and maybe to form words over supper, words such as *risen from ancient myths* (this makes me laugh, will always make me laugh), and later to fall asleep exhausted with curtains of white and midday light, and to wake up annoyed. And between the veils of annoyance to become blind to your many sons growing up, as might happen to my brother's wife, a fate no less moving than that of the martyrs further south, at least if you consider the sweet fearless faces in the orchards, destined to take on all the facial expressions they can handle, and to bear all the roles they can bear.

The serenaders on the terraces have little knowledge of this, and it is better this way. Released from ravines and damp ugly huts, may they forever remain with their beauty, with the lathed heavens, with the rejoicing of their harps, it is better for them, I know this tonight. The tin jugs on the washing table tonight are ascribing my life to me; my pain belongs to the door hinges and the distant voices two flights below, and all my desire belongs to the straw I feel under the sheets. How many skies will come down tonight and take my breath away once more before leaving it to me; how many droughts will wet my lips tonight before the rivers start their way towards me, in barrels and hauled by white oxen, between the low whitish walls of which we already spoke, and in the distance shielded by markets and villages, city halls and churches.

Oh, one night—does it suffice to acquire hunger and thirst? Already I can hear other trains approaching on the nearby tracks, how briefly will they stop here? The next travellers are on their way, to the monuments of martyrs further south. But perhaps, too, the next person who will awaken from his slumber here, still a bit dazed when someone hands him down his bag and suitcase, and who will stay—awaited by his brother and wife, maybe by the children too—for want of other places. Wherever there is a place, there is no other place. For him I want to be in the branches of the young trees lining the street up from the train station, for him I want to melt into the inaudible choirs that serve memory, and hide behind the scrawny grasses which rub against each other, and whisper to him: Give yourself one night, before you stay.

The Crossbeam

I wanted to settle down on a crossbeam. I wanted to know what a crossbeam is, but no one tells me. Someone said he heard it was part of a ship, but how does he know, where does he conduct his inquiries? Another told me it is an old synagogue-form, long out of use. It comes from the lowlands and it disappeared with them. A third replied, after thinking for a while, that he saw certain connections to floodplains. If I consider these answers together (three out of many, I've asked many people, and almost no one declined to answer), they begin to resonate with one another, but only slightly so. Certain similarities begin to glow, but after longer consideration, for example, if you change the sequence, they don't hold up. And this with regard to an object which is supposed to hold, perhaps even to rescue. Of course I could choose not to change the sequence, or stop considering it at a certain point, at exactly the point before the sequence is changed: to declare a certain grid pattern to be final, a shade-plant to be green. To let similarities be, the way they happen, there aren't many anyway. They will only proliferate. The areas between the lights, no matter how curled or shaded or unconquered, or even how slanted they are; they could all be called similar as the years go by. There are tacticians who would strongly confirm this: You have to build a fire where the wood is dry, build a camp when you can and so on. But then the question of naming appears again, the old dragon-cloud, and this I am afraid of. Is it a name or is it a heart, a testimony or a tendency to be healthy? Chants, or the invocation of chants? Wasn't it already despotic of me to break off my inquiries at a moment of exhaustion? Or not exhaustion but rather the exaltation with which I began to ask the question just after noon, with which I invoked it? Take the lady with the white felt dog: What is a crossbeam? She only stammered something and laughed before she got away. (While the tacticians, had they been there, with their quiet gaze and arms resting on my old windowsill, under the roof, would have surveyed the street.) But didn't she say something about picking plums in ancient cities? Wasn't this what she associated with my crossbeam, now that I think of it? But I omitted her whole answer: Vicinity of steeples, lower gardens with pickers and silken gloves possibly hanging down—all this I didn't mention. So this is how arbitrary my selection is. Pure despotism—I have omitted what I forgot. And then the triad. Indeed, it seems obvious: Three alleys where friends live, three Muslims, three tranquillities before making the leap. But isn't the triad also a result of despotism? Who would call a triangular plaza which opens up to a river a natural occurrence? Not even the locals. And there are families with five or six children who have often assured me: It would be the fourth. But I have chosen my crossbeam, and now I must live up to it. The question of despotism is certainly not the only one it raises, even if the question leads far afield and leaves room for diversions. For example, standpoints. What are those? A crossroad of gold and black lines close to the slaughterhouse? There won't be any more precise answers to that one. Because: I shake the shoulders of a stranger walking ahead of me, and I ask him—to his surprise—my old question. But where was he in that instant, where was he dwelling? In a gentle or in a desperate terrain, appropriate or inappropriate, leaning towards war games or not? What made him think of synagogues or floodplains, or parts of ships? Perhaps he could tell me, but it would be more accurate if he didn't. And even more accurate if I never asked to begin with. Also I don't want my first question to be displaced by a second one. What is a crossbeam? There it is again, and I will stick to it. I saddle the question, I adjust it just right, and I let it graze under the wispy birches and let it do what it wants. And even if it chases me into despotism's arms, which I fear, I can't escape it any more.

The only thing I could still ask is: How did I come to this question? Was it the slantedness, the wood? I always had a thing for smells. But this question would be disingenuous, and it would get me nowhere. I should let it go. What is a crossbeam? Swing wide, my dear question, and settle in the most suspicious nests, lure the wheezing greyhounds out of their dens. No one would have guessed how miserably greyhounds could live, all covered in rags, often very close to gardens, to the gardens' daily bloom. One should also consider this: Who not to ask? All moose breeds, stags and hinds—oh useless and endless to name them all. But the silence I evoke by not asking them: The unresponsiveness, how do I account for it?

On the other hand this lout, this young man I asked, ran away giggling. Son of a confectioner, a former soldier and all that, he didn't answer. Neither did his flour-dusted mother, she angrily threw me out of the shop. Anger and giggles, so that also counts. Slowly

I begin to be proud of my question, slowly it becomes a part of me and nestles in my bones, even if it harvests humiliation, or rather—especially if it does. For the question shouldn't become a song, certainly not, I don't want my voice to be softened with chalk, or was it flour? No, the streets with the pastry shops on the left will soon lie behind me, and behind them the Fields of Mars sprawl out, the sun with its pale white lies—this will help. There is little to choose from on the field, and if there is one lonely rebel moaning in the yellow grass the question will again be easy. He will point with his crooked fingers towards the remains of the battle, to the walls and stones, some still standing, and this is how he will help me. He will make me feel empty, he will make me feel heard, and both at the same time—only the most miserable can do this. Didn't they say synagogue? Very close. For these ruins lack distinct features, only the hours are still pointy. No more naves, flat or vaulted ceilings, no Feast of the Rosary to the left (but their absence speaks volumes). More like parts of a ship, rudders, barge wood, but only if you wish. From there to the floodplains it is only a short leap. Apparently even the confectioner's son couldn't put me on another track, his giggles, his mother's anger, her floured apron—everything was already part of it. So who could criticize me for being too straightforward? In relation to my question, sons of confectioners are certainly unusual, almost unsurpassably so. They only refer to themselves, and yet they are connected to solutions, to mites, to the hope of the world. What more could you want? Green roosters in nursing homes, once I saw one. It was lying on a woman's pillow, it was edible. And all this derives from the old white shelves. That's why I insist on my confectioner's boy, that's why I resist and I don't let ambition outwit me (there it is again, the triad), yes, I even bless the moment I first saw him in his short coat, thin and hunched forward, crossing the empty square. No idea where he was off to, not back to the soldiers, I guess. Flatfooted, with brooding eyes, and his Jewish wedding certificate in his pocket. No, certainly not to the soldiers. Though I would have liked to connect him to my poor hero; I would have grabbed him by the belt and said: Come, sit down beside him, and tell him some fairy tales! But this is not where we are headed. We've already lowered the probe too far into the splintered wood, now we must go on. We must follow the trace of bird hearts, the trace of fearlings. What is a crossbeam? Not: What is it to me. Rather: What is it? And if I had followed the lady with the felt dog and the plum orchards, what sequence would I have found? Would her overloaded gardens (I'm sure she meant overladen) have led us to synagogues, to ship wood? Probably not. Pickers are like beams that run length-wise. And neither would they have led us to the near floodgates, to the slow wind. Or to stinking passageways. But then would I have been open enough to find the floodplains? Already they are dancing and fading before my eyes, the lesser and lazier possibilities, clouding my mind like unknown relatives, mildly mellow folks. No sequences, no sorrow, no obliterating thoughts. Such possibilities. But I know I'm imagining them. Sorrow will come, no matter who I address my question to, and obliteration too. Sure, I've followed the son of the confectioner, followed the losers, the loose giggles, the pox-covered dying; I've let the flour that no one needed dust the way behind me. But if I hadn't done it, if I had contented myself with more harmless notions, what would ever change? (Those tacticians with their discreet grins.) What is a crossbeam? The lady wouldn't have led me anywhere else either. Therefore I stick to it, with my grey sequence, my choice, my despotism: synagogues, ship wood, floodplains. The results of one day. And not because I agree with the tacticians, certainly not. They barely use their voices.

Earmarks, hallmarks, someone whispered to me, a gift. Isn't this rather unsubstantial? The way the vowels sound slightly similar? Their elegant sequence, the way they try to rope each other in? I won't be led to that. Gift, gift? Sounds too much like splinters, it leads far afield. Like license-holders, like garden warblers. Someone might as well come and point me towards the darkest passageways. (To the yards of state prisons, for example, where the gallows stand.) No, I will stick to my weak responses. And to my question. Not: Where does it come from. Not: Earmarks, hallmarks. I know them well enough. But rather: What is it? Because I don't want to name it any more.

II

Memories for Samuel Greenberg

1

I saw the emperor. The emperor was wrapped in blue paper. Sometimes he was also surrounded by pheasants. He bent down to me. When he tried to give me his hand, I began to cry. I cried so loudly that I made the emperor vanish.

2

He came down the stairs. He emerged hunched over between the shelves. The people moved aside. He motioned them to stay. Someone tried a piano concerto on a cello. The emperor took the sheet of music and held it closer to the musician. The place was fumigated.

3

It might also have been a cargo ship. Inside it, a small library, or at least book stands. One member of the crew was always on duty. He lay grumpily in the corner. The emperor dropped by but he didn't borrow a book. Now enough of the emperor.

4

Let us begin. Everything seemed gold and orange to me. Even the cabbage heads were submerged in lush morning light. They were carrying one of their high-minded people to the grave. Instead of four pallbearers he had five, his bier swayed on long sticks, he lay there uncovered. The whole thing looked Chinese.

5

My father got a hold of me. Stay here, stay here, he shouted, just stay here. Don't you dare join them. You're already my fifth. And so I stayed.

6

But I was turned to the side, so no one could set me straight. And no one needed me, either. I was an off-spring, a form of gossip. I always looked behind me. And if someone wanted me to stop watching the underpasses, he would have had to motion me to go through them. And no one wanted that, either.

7

So everything stayed the way it was. I proceeded straight ahead, but I set my sight on the margins, all

kind of margins, impoverished and otherwise. If someone from the margins smiled at me, I was already gone.
My feet carried me further, isn't that what they say?

8

Then came the funeral again with the five sticks. And
my father again. One knows the drill. One gets better
at it, every time. Every smoke hits home.

9

But it's no use, we have to be on our way.

10

We must go away.

Port Sing

Port Sing, where the hares rest. They all have a tendency to disappear, but here they rest, nobody knows why. It could have happened this way: when the first unscrupulous settlers landed with their rafts and put them ashore—perhaps even forcing them to jump—and pushed off again, the hares didn't see anything better, nothing that attracted them more. Thus they began to burrow into the flat hollows on the beach and to watch the grainy yellow hills and the needleless pines, features of the bay. It wasn't hard to picture what lay beyond, even if the picture turned out to be wrong. A resting place was created. When the rains began, which mostly fell sideways and from the south, the hares managed to slow their movements. When it began to hail, they lay in the wet sand, resembling blocks, changing their colour. The settlers or former rafters who were now pressing their cheeks against the portholes far out at sea on their ships never took them for hares, and so most continued to float quickly past the bay, even against the wind. When summer reached the hares with reddish nettles and grapes and it began to dawn on them that their numbers had grown, the older ones climbed up the bank and disappeared into the hinterlands. One could imagine that they founded the city of Nîmes there, but the opposite is easy to prove. The hares weren't interested in founding cities, while their opponents were interested in keeping them from founding cities. Linen makers and root growers possibly gathered soon in front of the imagined walls and began to shoot—they mastered that early on. They stood next to each other in one line, a mysterious sight. Soon afterwards they began to build their bright rectangular buildings which were riddled with holes. The hares remained outside. In their own blood, in the bushes, in the entrails, where remaining is inevitable. This was the fate of the older ones. The younger hares didn't know what to do with the sounds from the hinterlands. Sounds in general were foreign to them. They mastered the grounds and the gifts of the bay, its sights and fluctuations from yellow to green, its soundlessness; this is where they felt at home. They could have—if they had been aware of it—practised deafness, its forms and detours, and with it they could more easily have measured the moment of disappearance than with their limping legs and ears. But this is how it was, one has to make do even with imperfect mistakes. The hares made do. They had enough strength left to climb up the banks without help. They slowly started to replace their early shaky circles—which they had all dug into the sand close to the cliff—with rigorous, more isolated forms, and if they took this for a sign none of them let it show. Signs were abundant, even in what doubtlessly surrounded them there were plenty of signs. After approximately a hundred and three years, the rumour of the city of Nîmes began to spread, and to this day it hasn't been proven. It may very well stem from the misunderstood shouts of the day trippers, all this nonsense at sea. Someone there testing his voice—does it reach the bay, or does it not reach the bay? It doesn't reach the bay, but it's sufficient to imagine a medium-sized city with town walls, hat stands and all that. Or was it because of the sand? It flew up and one of the hares understood it. But you hares are not supposed to understand, what do you think your ears are for? Too late. After a hundred and five years, the hares became restless, they converged at unused spots in the sand, and sometimes a younger hare had to help an older hare up the bank. Deed and misdeed mingled, the rumour of the duchesses was created, Valentine and Hortense, or whatever their names were, and it couldn't be stopped. The two existed and examined themselves in the mirror, they held their bonnets over clear and brackish water and ordered yellow leaves to be cut if they were running out of leaves; their silken skirts trailed through the bay. The hares had never seen anything like it, and their fear grew, and with it a voice and a desire to climb the trees that bordered the back of the bay, which were really only bushes; and so royal councils were summoned and they all sat in a circle with the merry duchesses in the middle. The holy mountain was mentioned, its blue and green colours destined to clean the world, and a decision was made to set out—pieces of advice began to darken every inlet of the bay. One of the duchesses owned a glass ball on top of a wooden stick in the sand. When they set out it was carried in the front, but it shattered against a pine tree before the top of the bank was reached. The light is gone, they all shouted; the hares turned back and stayed—can you blame them? Wasn't staying the only thing that couldn't wait? From then on, flickering lights illuminated the bay: shards of the shattered ball. Nobody cleaned them up; instead they were honoured and fenced in. For the younger hares, they were the only sign of reassurance. The duchesses took off, probably to Nîmes, which at this point must have already been in existence, or close to its transformation from idea to appealing place. Certainly they did their part whenever the transformation proved difficult—with their dances in courtyards, which were growing in number, or by unsettling the open fields. Accounts have been preserved about these dances, by goat herders and light-board operators, but nothing certain. No one followed their example. The walls of Nîmes grew, yellow and whitish, and only the hares cared about the holy mountain. They invented directions and precipices and path widths, they specified danger zones and began to let more and more colours in. They garnered hope from imagined valleys, ellipses and heart shapes covered with winter fog that made everything imagined and black stand out more clearly, if only because of the dampness. They even started talking about rules for harvesting the shoots of pine trees on the lower slopes or foothills of the holy mountain. The sand under their soles proved helpful to their plots; they remained in the bay. Valentine and Hortense, the duchesses, never reappeared, and the shadows of Nîmes no longer came disturbingly close. Two more times the hares were bothered by humans: once when a mill was erected not far from the bay with sails attached so clumsily that one of the strong eastern storms blew them onto the beach; the other time thirty-five years later when an old beggar staggered down the bank only to die in their midst. One of the fenced-in glass shards was slightly displaced on this occasion, and from then on everything was quiet. For five or six centuries nothing happened, the new directions were observed with craft and courage, at times a rosy light spread over the sand, a smell of corn drifted down from the bank. But dances, eastern storms, beggars, the smell of corn—is this what it was all about, for them? One early afternoon the hares departed to the holy mountain, a departure that wasn't entirely unexpected. It had been predicted seven decades before by a movement which soon died out, but needs to be mentioned nevertheless: a few hares had gone into the sea. The Mirror Fencers (an old and powerful sect that around the same time had sent boats past the bay, at a proper distance) offered peculiar explanations. One: There were too many hares. Second: They didn't have enough food. None of these explanations proved right or was even worth debating; the hares pulled themselves together soon enough and the seaward groups began to hesitate. It was the light of the shards—resembling, with their circular fences, trees on boulevards—which gave them consolation, or disconsolation enough. They had grown used to the fact that the sick died in their midst. Not one single hare had gone over the bank during the last nine decades before their departure—neither life nor death nor anything had given them enough reason to. Then they all went. One can't say that it was a special day or afternoon: it had begun like many others—namely, not at all—and it hovered over the bay, paralysing and mobilizing, and it didn't offer reasons. It was simply time. Carefully they walked past the shards near the bank—and for many hares the moment they got close to them, to their faded yellowish and rosy glow, was the surprise of their lives. As might be expected, what was not a surprise was the top of the bank, the ferns that had settled there, the lowlands that spread out in front of them, the shadows of the distance. From now on their moments could no longer be described with jumps, but however new this was to them, they didn't notice. They avoided looking right, for that was where Nîmes might have been, and they rested under trees. They met a soldier with a grey-red tricorn, a peasant woman and a harlequin whom they didn't recognize as a harlequin. Fine with us, they might have thought. Enough. Which meant a lot for them, for their short new lives. Thoughts like these tuned their minds calmly, preparing the ground for new names. *Cabbage knife*, one hare said, and pointed to a signpost, but even he wasn't greeted with exaggerated attention. *Temple traverses,* some hares named the country roads that led to nothing but piles of corn straw. Let's not get side-tracked by examples—they advanced quickly. The mumbling, the short whistling sounds, the shuffling and whispering which was supposed to bolster the sick among them was picked up by a few soft gusts of wind and carried away but not necessarily towards the holy mountain. The rumours of sun portals and paths multiplied, leaving everything to be desired. Nîmes, if it even existed, lay far behind them, with its imaginary smooth trenches, tombs and monuments; and no more corn braiders and harlequins came. The hares didn't mind. No master was born from the fields, wringing his hands, or sheepishly wiping them off on his rough, stitched cloth. Instead a wide blue-green strip of light began to spread quickly, covering savoury and rye, heaven and hell, and the pieces of wood in front of them. The hares dwelt in it—disturbing coloured lights were nothing new to them, and the dusty cloud around the lights, tinted and shrinking, seemed to advance briskly. Shortly after they had to bury the first exhausted hares. And what certain

47

observers would have revelled in is the fact that their pauses of burials and rest seemed to follow a rule, they occurred in a pattern, and thus—according to the impartial bystanders—neared necessity. Almost like flying, they would have thought. Almost flight, yes. The mountain range was now so close that it no longer had an outline. Let's not waste time with the ascent. The hares' feet were unable to adjust quickly to piles of ice and grit, to drifting cushions of pine needles and unexpected plunges. And so all sorts of things were swirling around in the zephyr of the holy mountain which hardly resembled rocks or blocks. But it was a fine day, no screams; except for the falls there was nothing that wasn't restrained, or softened, or soothed. This was the invention of huskiness. Everything was abyss, a gorge without an opposite wall. The bank proved to be an insufficient test for climbing the mountain (the proximity of the fenced-in shards was probably only a foretaste of the falls), but for the end it certainly sufficed. Its low height was key. We remember: ferns, flatlands and Nîmes which no one looked at.

Four hares stepped on to the peak of the holy mountain. There'd been a burning smell in the air, but it didn't stop them, bravely they wrestled through low shrubs. But what did they decide when they saw the fiery gorge? Did they settle at its edge, did they eat something? Were there springs near, or liquids that would have favoured the building of dens? Who wouldn't have liked to witness the hares at this point, heads tucked together, paws singed? Who wouldn't have liked to come too close, one final time? But no one is allowed. Then are we allowed to speak of hares when there are only four left? What number protects a name? No, none of us can ever shake off this question: Were we ever allowed to speak of hares? Or of Port Sing?

Five Proposals

I propose a lady in a grey dress, with a red collar on it. Nothing shall be divided. Not the collar and not the dress. Nothing that is not predetermined shall be predetermined. Birdlike, but not forcefully so, that's how she is best described. She needs to be able to climb stairs, up and down, to pause and turn, many skills. And to be rewound and covered with lacquer. The edges often go unmeasured, no one wants to do it. I'm not a tool, the lady often says. That doesn't make it easier for her to appear. Preparing for winter has never concerned her. I have enough bast, she says disdainfully. Now it is society's turn to be surprised. Step by step, keeping up with sleep, it is good this way. There are enough objections already. She walks stiltedly, she has no feet, hence the bast. And her hair is not in order. Yarn, wool, thread, unwound, worked up, undone again, nothing compares to it. That's always a curse. And the colour fluctuates during thunderstorms. Sometimes she meets Emperor Ferdinand outside the village. Always in the north, who knows how she gets there? One can see: nothing is simple about her except the dress and perhaps her feet. I therefore apologize for the red collar. I proposed it, just as I proposed her. But I can already hear opposing voices, bolder proposals, pronounced opinions. To be so quickly misunderstood borders on homage. They misunderstand me, but I don't want to insist. I was just thinking.

With Emperor Ferdinand it's different. He wears light blue, he crosses the streets quickly and always diagonally, and he admires details, even on the frontlines. He gives away his meeting spots: the gates and wells. This is rather incompetent because there's always someone behind him, be it the French or the Americans of the north-west. But he spends his nights in small damp rooms. It keeps him young, and the fleeing earth doesn't unsettle him. He says he prefers to take steep paths upward rather than downward. What paths? Mountain paths. Are there other ones? Certainly. Level ones, with scrawny ranunculi left and right. Oh, those. He doesn't use those at all. Once he did, but that was as a private person. Purely private. Can he swear to that? He can. But he's hard to catch up with. Before you suspect anything, you are already ahead of him and then he is untraceable, talking to farmers in the bushes—while you rush breathlessly through the mountain peaks in the foreground—about the condition of the wood and about latifundia. He takes the condition of wood seriously, this makes him tricky. He's not an easy emperor, he's often ahead of us. Too speedy for imperial norms, and in his speed, too thoughtful. Some people confirm this. We'll drop him.

An epic in the form of roses. I mean: roses mixed among verses. Vouched for, and the roses clearly visible. Otherwise, people will disapprove. Not reliable, they will say, and write it in their grievances. Or they will write: When I recently rushed by your shop window, there was no rose in the centre. But doesn't the basic rule also allow for off-centre showcasing, or showcasing in shadows, and call for passers-by to have stronger eyesight? We need to follow up on this: We need to include optometrists. But what for? Who relies on such excuses? In that case, why not use green poles instead of poles wrapped in green? That's it—and the excuses we make for losers are the most entertaining thing about the basic rule. But then why not fasten the roses with lacquer instead of using their growth? That's it, that's it. And let's be honest: How often was natural growth used in emergencies as a default nail to hang your argument on? A fine epic. Did I say that? I said: Shadows and off-centre showcasing are good enough, if not specifically invented for this purpose. And let's assume someone has too many eyeglass lenses or too much green in his store, and can't get rid of it, and suddenly doesn't want to get rid of it any more because he feels pity. What else should he do but carefully seek out the peripheries? And what becomes of the roses in the end? They are received. With growth, or nails, or lacquer mixed in, it doesn't matter. Received and dismissed. Welcomed and let go. Aha.

Or smallpox at mare time. You'll have to give me more details, I don't know anything about that. What are mares? Horses. And mare time? Horse time. Special horses? No, not special, heavy hoofs and short manes. Shaft horses, maybe. Can they turn sharply? No. Then there are no crooked roads? No, no crooked roads. Poor horses! Poor horses? How about the ears? Long but already grey. And pointed at the top, which helps with deafness. Does that create a sense of self? Not really. But the hoofs. Yes, the hoofs are the crucial point. Too heavy? Perhaps too heavy. Does that weigh them down? It weighs them down heavily. And every horse? Almost every one. But the smallpox? The smallpox? I mean the mares. Why the mares? The manes, I mean. Oh, I see, they are thin, and short, as I said before. They always fall out. Because of the bugs? No, just like that, a lightness, and the street is covered with mane hair as if it were hemp. And can the mane hair be used to make ropes? It breaks easily. But that's bad for the population. For whom? I mean it's bad. Bad it is. It's easy to slip, head over heels and so forth. Who falls head over heels? The horses who walk over it with their shaft poles. Do they try to get up again? They try. And do they succeed? Not all of them. And so a confusion breaks out on the ground and beyond. Then the small-pox comes. All the way here! And here the shaft poles break, and everything shifts in a different direction than usual. Luckily they are mares. Luckily? With their skinny ribs, almost falling off. I mean, couldn't they brush off the pox, on the sides? On the barren pines left and right? There are no barren pine trees. Now forgive the nosy question: What colour are the pock-marks? They are black. Then couldn't everything be changed? Changed? I mean: Smallpox at mare-time? Doesn't this fall a bit short? This we need to consider.

And finally let's try little Edison, who hangs around in our shed. He took three blue pencils from his drawer, and now he always carries them around. He draws on barrel staves. What does he draw? First off, three pencils, and pencils are difficult to draw. Whoever doesn't know this should be warned not even to try. Whoever knows this should lead the way. Difficult to draw—but what, exactly? Starting with the tip: Everything. The edges, six corners, sometimes eight, the length. And furthermore the weight of cobwebs and dampness, perhaps of sleep. And always the blue in the eye. One must be able to imagine this. Why doesn't little Edison go home? Now he's come to this spot. Not too much effort with the steps. When the Nile and the other streams behind the knotholes come into sight: only the necessary movements. But he doesn't see the Nile. No, he doesn't see the Nile. But you've got to give him time. His mother is waiting, and the hungry Egyptians. There are many things that little Edison wouldn't dream of. Maybe we'll choose him.

Only Joshua

Only Joshua can be helped. He knows how to enter boats and how to leave them again, he oversees the floodlands, he tries his hand with emigrés. There is nothing he hasn't tried his hand at. He is the one we need to get a hold of, the one we need to bestow with appropriate assets, with family, with an empty spot. Out of thin air he conjures everything from these spots. If need be: kitchen pails, stirring spoons, double beeches. His vision is unobstructed. Chests are not foreign to him either—carved, painted, handmade, rough or lacquered, the boat-shaped hideouts, single chests for entry halls and the more complex ones for upstairs. Quickly he rushes up the stairs and shifts wicker chairs, leans on windowsills—now with his back towards us— and measures the land, dividing up pastures, ordering barbed wire and turnstiles for the shepherds. When the beeches start to grow, the calves will have matured. The barren garden does not justify his vision yet, but tomorrow it will. Joshua pictures benches and women, he hears the ancient melody from open summer windows, sung in three voices, full. There they are coming from the marshland with their baskets, laughing, manoeuvring over planks, waving. Tell me, tell us, Joshua says, and turns away. And now sons arrive, born from a short turn or turn of phrase, and primroses and wild strawberries. Joshua is the one: he understands that turning away can be useful, he builds on that. Now we need to help him go further. Maybe with a barge for the waste water—now he's the one waving. He stands there, legs spread wide, accompanied by sobs, or shall we say stork cries. Yes, stork cries. Who tells him all these things? How to jump off, how to sell old barges, how to suck on breasts? Who approves of him? Now there are daughters waiting by the planks, he bends down, he has a grey beard, he could easily be set in marble, simply the way he is standing right now, almost mid-leap. Thus they lead him into the house, and everything is there again, marble sinks, hunting tales, scenes in relief. He needs to lower his head when he walks through the portals. Someone called him a stallion, but he is not, he will forever be a mariner. He's gentle with the little ones, that's how he gets by on land, he sinks his gaze into the moor-shapes which look like embroidery; he fishes out the soldiers. Once he found a whip snake and hung it round his neck, the whole company laughed. Once he drew the Last Judgement as a triangle into the rock with his foot. He is right-footed. They wanted to hire him for gravestones since he's so strong, but he prefers not to. It's not his kind of thing. He prefers small forts, where the postcard sellers put him on their signs, then he greets the orthodox when they come visit, this sort of thing suits him better. He lifts his face into the air then, smiling and upturned, cheerful enough. Back in their homelands, the orthodox keep thinking of him. A wax taper preserves his features for ever. A kitchen maid dies crying in his honour and is buried under matthiola, four names. A sun flies up. The clay cracks. And yet the potherbs thrive and raise their heads, the colour of the walls changes in stages. Where shall he be erected, the dear hero, he who is so similar to the sand fleas that stabilize the shore? Another man already stands in front of the sundial, father of the country, explorer, patron of the stronger third of the world's oceans. He can't be moved. Who would have thought that one day our Joshua would lean around awkwardly, looking for crampons, for a spot in this town? Even a cellar would suffice for him to be stored properly, transported by hands. Bright places are rare, he understands that. Difficult to share them with others. Then he much prefers the embroidery circles in cellars and the quiet patter of beginner groups above. One day he will surely enter the tapestries and remain there for ever, smiling, eating from the spit, being looked at. Beginners learn quickly, that is a proven fact. First the evening red and then the rest; grey nests are more difficult, but he doesn't need them anyway. Nothing rat-coloured except under the heels, that's how they do it. Late Gallic. The decades will bring him out, singing with cannons of light. Our dear Joshua.

The Jouet Sisters

Now I only keep company with the two Jouet sisters. They caution me when I exaggerate. When I say *farmstead* instead of *farm*, for example, they instantly jump on it. You did it again, says Rosalie. She calls Anna and Josepha, and we start over. *A junk*, says Rosalie, *a junk* I say. *China*, shouts Anna, *China* I shout. *Foxes*, says Josepha, the quiet one. *Joshua* I say. We have to start again. *Jonah*, says Josepha, *Jonah* I say. *Jonah*, says Anna, *Jonah* I say. *Jonah*, says Rosalie. Now leave me alone, I say. And again. Are there three sisters? Yes, there are three. I now only keep company with the three Jouet sisters. *Ragtag*, I say to enrage them. *Ragtag*, says Anna. *Predatory hordes. Predatory hordes*, repeats Josepha. *Diligence at school, diligence in general, diligence in particular*, I say quickly. *Diligence at school, diligence in general, diligence in particular*, says Rosalie. *But not alone*, I say. They are silent. *Tent, tent*, I shout. Nothing. I bend over my writing again. *Tent?* No, not *tent*, they don't know a thing about tents. *Foreign regions*, I shout over their heads. *Foreign regions*, Rosalie repeats hesitatingly, *foreign regions*, says Josepha too quietly, one can barely understand her. I need to turn to other themes, perhaps theme parks? Too meagre. Or parks for hunters. Leather stools, English rifles. Or embroidery tools? I can't decide. My pen drips, the Jouet sisters are looking at me. Now I have it—we need school utensils, notebooks, binders, West African history between cardboard covers. But I have no words for that, not a sound. They look at me, these sisters, and I don't contribute anything. But this landscape is about contributions, that ought to be clear. And it needs to be clear beforehand, before the letters, before everything else. Contributions are customary here. And only then comes flora, and then fauna, and whatever else emerges, snake islands, borders being drawn, most of it open to negotiation, and easily stored under the cover of beeches. I saw a flock of cranes, in formation, caught in the act of flying, stuffed with feathers, nailed on wooden stands. In perfect formation, not an easy task. A beautiful flock. Rosalie would say so, too. If she felt like saying it. Rosalie is blonde. She has thin hair and wears it parted like her grandmother in the motherland. What am I saying? We never want to speak of that, I will comply, it's not too hard. Anna and Josepha no longer remember anything, they are dark and look straight ahead. When they talk

61

to me they place themselves right in front of me; Rosalie doesn't need to do that. She brushes my shoulders, she speaks from the roof, from the soiled monuments, from behind corn barrels. The motherland, what a joke, we'll leave that for now. When Rosalie goes into the desert, the border guards under their burnouses take notice, but they don't dare say anything. Rosalie often goes into the desert. I could fancy that she does it for the sand, for my writing. She carries the sand in her Chinese children's pail. The sand is her pretext, the reason she gives me. For her the desert walks will have other reasons, her own reasons. She collects nutshells, says Josepha and looks straight at me. She keeps the desert in order. She gives drawing lessons, shouts Anna, she took me with her twice. She taught me how to draw the swan and the duck. The species, says Josepha. Naturally the species, answers Anna absentmindedly. With hooks in their boots, black patent leather from home.

Home. Home? *Mein Land.* There was a crash when we came home. I mean, came here, every time, both times, there was a crunching sound in our stockings, yes, there was. We'll be happy to take this on ourselves, says Josepha, won't we, Rosalie? *On* ourselves, I say. *On* ourselves, I like it, I'll take it. *On* ourselves. What do you mean? says Rosalie. This is how she is. A teacher of deserts, in drawings. And then web-footed birds. With all the collected nutshells as fins. *Fin school*, I shout, *fin school*, I shout now and clap my hands. I know I have no clue about after-school programmes but I should, I should feel like a dream and value cleanliness, that would be fitting. *The sand from the shoes,* I should shout, and after an appropriate minute, *pass your teacher the salt, Josepha.* Or *Anna.* Or *Anna too.* But I don't—I take my Jouet sisters as they are, kind as they are towards beggar women at the desert's edge, sometimes without charm. As an arbour, as a dry desert wind, a heart-shaped leaf. Or leaves. As a company. Threefold. We never go fishing together. No game preserves. Nothing but my exaggerations which hold us together. That's why I mustn't abandon them, I must attend to my desk and continue to write my reports to the motherland about the land, about the motherland to the land. In-between, there is *naufrage.* These are the threads. *Here the bricks sink into the soil,* one of my reports reads, I thought of that all by myself. *There the straw blows away,* reads another, and I simply believe it. I saw it blow away with my eyes closed. There were also travellers who reported this. *You won't believe how the straw blows away over there,* they said, and drove away.

Especially on the West Coast. My pen scratches, it's my first pen. Don't exaggerate, says Rosalie. Don't exaggerate, says Anna. It's your second. What? Oh, yes. Your second, says Josepha soothingly, rustling her grey dress, *your second pen.* Naturally. Shortly afterwards I see her cowering at the leg of my table, picking at old gauze. You broke the first pen when we escaped the cannibals. I know, I know. *Your second peace.* My second peace, who says that? Josepha said it. Josepha? It is my third peace, Josepha. *Poor Jonah,* says Josepha gently. This is surprising. Since I was washed ashore no one has called me that. No man should be called poor if he can make do with his eating utensils. Or with his shoulders, or his sense of smell. Then we would have to say poor Samson, you have only one nose—but we don't say that. And I did have silverware in my bread sack. A complete set. From time to time Josepha polishes it, she sits down on the temple porch and rubs it. With her association of a Chinese junk. Once, a compote spoon got lost, maybe that's what she meant. In any case, it glows more strongly now than during our childhood days by the river, it glows stronger than ever. And then I rarely eat compote, the water here is too brackish, many kinds of fruits and fruit sugars perish in it. But one can make do with cattle, with lions' eyes and a hint of dill. Rosalie laughs. She gathered the dill. With her sister Anna, it wasn't dill. We all ate it. *Help yourself, sir,* the three of them said, *have some, go ahead.* The table was set brilliantly. Completely in white, a half-tropical kind of forget-me-not tied to every fork for the preservation of this particular variety. We are making do. Around every piece of silverware there was a silken thread from the motherland, but I should not mention it. There are no female spinners here, the white fathers hold them back. *Rain,* says Anna and gets to work on the roof. *Rain,* says Rosalie, *rain* says Josepha. With one voice and it starts falling from the sky. Wouldn't that suit you just fine? To be tense, to listen and to sleep intently, to let the jewellery be rained on, my dear sisters, you would like that but I wouldn't. Why are you called Jouet? Are there districts where you come from, divine guests of the ancient sort? Do the fish contain iodine? What inspired your father to each of you? And what inspired him to himself? I am alone without you. I have only you on my mind. Why are you so grey, rosy, orange, blue and the rest? So devoted, as if you had no choice? Or do you think I exaggerate again, Rosalie? Do you think so, Anna? Do you think so, Josepha? Do I exaggerate? Am I rash, frivolous? Is that what one calls it? I should say *rain* and let it patter. Low shrubbery, mission schools, beacon fires in the mud, everything will be equally undermined. *Rain,* I should repeat after you and eagerly breathe in the wetness, just like the relatives on your father's side as soon as they intuited the painted dining rooms, long before your time. As soon as their automatic water pipes in the yard stopped working, which was soon. *Presently, inventively, opaquely* said someone with the names of *Boote*, he knows these things, a cousin of your great uncle, he didn't take after you. Let him be, he likes to hang around by the fires. These old addendums, what's one to do with them? They are mashed into a pulp, and right away they begin to grow and age again. Fire, fires, scarred ground, hanging white, yes. Legitimately, there it is again. With both boots on the ground of riverbeds, and the rivers named after generals, and the riverbeds breeding ground for hookworms, everything mapped out, I know, and I will now shut up. I lean towards my sisters who are grey and white. Who have no legs but can walk and can tear out the traps set for desert foxes, who is that? You, my dears. The Jouets were pleasant, people will say of you. All three were very pleasant, they will say. Is that really what you want? They had church-run plantations where no one would expect them, near Schaffhausen, for example. They drank up the water for those who were drowning. They were good at playing the piano with six hands. What else did people say? They were devoted. Now you know. The desert foxes which you saved, they are digging you out, into the light. Devoted, what do you say to that? Gathered around a man who could have been their father. Devoted. I won't comment, I only wait for what you have to say, from now on this is all I'm waiting for. What you say, I say. What do you say? *School building?* Very good. *School building,* says Rosalie, *school building,* says Anna, *school building,* says Josepha. *Joseph's house,* says Rosalie. *With windows.* What else is to come? Table and uniform, velar or labial sounds, secrets, seal-hunting? I'm waiting, I'm waiting—for monkey bread and peanuts, for cotton balls, pastry and the heroes of the fatherland. For Ascension Day and its one-way mission to heaven. My sweet doves, my wooden lights. How can I say amen before you say it?

My Language and I

My language is one that tends towards foreign words. I choose them, I retrieve them from far away. But it is a small language. It doesn't reach far. All around, all around me, always all around and so forth. We advance against our will. To hell with us, I sometimes say to it. It turns, it doesn't answer, it lets us happen. Sometimes Customs officers appear. Your passports? We pass, they let us pass. My language didn't say anything, but I did, I nodded obligingly, I did them this favour. One person, and something around him, unsuspicious. But what was around him? A coiled spring. No, smoke. There is something around everyone, don't you know this? These poor boys, I honestly feel sorry for them. Honestly. Now you're babbling. What do they have or not have that makes you feel sorry? They're young, that's all—what's there to feel sorry about? They'll grow, that's inevitable. They will get powerful and they will become a force. While we remain stuck in the ink, like a farce, slaving away, pretending to be cheerful—while we're losing our cheerfulness. Honestly. Who is that, who says that? Me. This cracks me up. This always reminds me of the one who said Me!, when he arrived too late at his own house and wanted to be let inside. I am reminded of him, what was his profession? Custodian, I believe. Yes, custodian. Are you hungry? Because I definitely am. But I have this habit of always omitting one hunger. First one, then two, then three. But then there will be a meal, I swear, where nothing is omitted, where everything will be on the table, spread out before me. Then they all cavort around, all around me, and then I have it. Sleepy? Well sleep, go ahead and sleep. I'll keep watch for you.

This is where I sit with my language, only 3 metres away from the people who talk like that. But we made it through, we have passed, we can take a rest when we are out of breath. There are plenty of empty spots, put a blanket down, the sun shines everywhere. My language and I, we don't talk to each other, we have nothing to say to each other. I know what I have to know—it likes cold food better than warm food, not even the coffee should be hot. This can really keep you busy. It's a lot of work, laying out the plates, cutting the food, measuring the cold, letting the warmth dis-sipate. While my language stares out at the sea. It's easy for my language to stare, because I do everything. I don't rush like I used to, I now calmly smooth the blanket, I calmly weight it with stones when it gets windy, but it's true: I work and it stares. It doesn't even express wishes. This wouldn't be the utmost one could ask of it, but it would be something. A good deed, a service to me, a way to help me progress. But my language doesn't care, that much I understand. It only stares or listens to the surf, my language. I make sure that we are always near the sea. I, not it. I would like to know what would happen to my language if one day I walked inland, if I simply took a turn like other people do, picking a stone table for us between the hollows, the shaved pines. What would it do then— would it come with me? The coastal wind is bad for my ears, this much I know. Sometimes I begin to sing, or to bang the silverware, then everything becomes quieter. Even though our kind of food doesn't require utensils, I unpack the silverware, the plates and glasses, too. I hold up a knife and then I let it fall, carefully, on the plate, always from the same height. For five weeks now everything has been getting quieter. Recently I tried to let the knife fall on the plate from a slightly higher distance. It banged loudly, I heard it clearly, but the plate broke. My language remained calm, its gaze pinned on the sea, always, I believe, on the same spot.

It seems to be the opposite of certain paintings where the gaze follows you everywhere—its gaze follows no one. Sea monsters and fishing boats would be equally lost on it. And none come anyway. At some point I begin to set out our cold meal, I pour the cold coffee, but in vain. Carefully I've set everything on our blanket, I even placed a coastal flower in the middle or right next to its plate. But my language doesn't turn around. I then put the plate in front of my language—right between it and the sea foam. My joy is gone, the hearing test has dampened my spirits, and the sea annoys me. My language used to have a lavender shawl, but it's gone. I fear we might ruin our health in this place. If my language loses its voice, then it has one more reason to stop talking to me. While I continue to besiege it with questions and offers—whispering, coughing. The lavender shawl looked good on my language, it covered its overly long neck and gave its unspoken appearance both gentleness and resoluteness. Now all of that's gone and my language doesn't even turn its collar up. The way it looks now, it sometimes reminds me of a mature swan but very dull in colour, as if its maturation were still ahead of it. But it shouldn't flatter itself. From afar I hear the voices of the Customs officers. They talk and talk, or at least one

71

of them is always talking. It wasn't my idea to settle down so close to the Customs booth, but my language refused to go further. The fourth country has ended, I shouted in its ear, the fifth is right over there. It followed me reluctantly—and no further than right here. The truth is, we might as well be Customs officers. Among them, only one does the talking, too—about food and youth while the other sleeps or stares at us through the windows, like right now. Earlier, when I searched for our passports, he was sleeping. I don't let my language carry our passports any more since it lost its shawl, I have them now.

They are bored over there. Or maybe they find us suspicious. They find my language suspicious, not me. I am normal, I eat and drink, and when I let the knife fall on the plate it doesn't look to them—at such a distance—like a hearing test, it looks like clumsiness, and that's quite all right with me. But if we stay longer, it will stop looking like clumsiness and will start to look like intent. If only my language talked to me, then I wouldn't need this kind of hearing test, but it does very little to keep us free of suspicion. Not even for my sake. It should really care more about me but I suspect it of only caring about itself. Or not caring about itself at all. Or both—how convenient. My language didn't touch what I put out, it lets sea foam salt its food. Each to his own, I think. I can also take others for my own. Or mistake them. I can become a Customs chef, a Customs entertainer, Customs officer. The two over there will not ignore what I put in front of them. We will talk about Customs, about Customs items, silver and lead and similar things. About card games—I also know card games. And about my language, which I suspect will never move away from here. From its salty meal, its grey gaze. I will do what I can for it. The talking alone will help, the conversations about it, the observations which will soon repeat themselves. In time, no one will want anything from my language. And I will do my part. I will weave in a sentence here and there to make it free of suspicion.

BAD WORDS

I

Bad Words

I now no longer use the better words. *The rain which pounds against the windows.* In the past I might have thought of something quite different. But enough of that now. *The rain which pounds against the windows.* That's sufficient. I just had another expression on the tip of my tongue—not only was it better, it was also more precise, but I forgot it while the rain was pounding against the windows or while the rain was doing what I was about to forget. I am not very eager to know what will occur to me during the next light rain, the next heavy rain—I suppose I will make do with one phrase for all types of rain. I won't care whether you can say *pound* when it only gently touches the windowpanes—or if that would be saying too much. Or too little, if the rain threatens to shatter the windows. I'll leave it at that for now. I'll stick with *pound*—let others worry about the rest.

To drag the downfall in front of yourself, I also thought of this, and certainly this phrase seems even more indefensible than pounding rain, because you never drag anything in front of yourself, you shove it, or push it—carts, for example, or wheel chairs; whereas other things such as potato sacks are dragged behind. Other things, certainly not downfalls. Those are transported in a different manner. I know this, and again the better phrase for this was just on the tip of my tongue, only to escape me. I don't mourn its loss. *To drag the downfall in front of yourself*, or better yet: *the downfalls*, I won't insist on either, but I'll stick to it. Can one say *I decide on it*—this is questionable. The standard usage doesn't make room for decisions where there's merely a possibility. Surely you could discuss this but I'm fed up with those discussions—they are mostly conducted in taxis on the way out of town—and thus I make do with my indefensible expressions.

Of course I won't be able to use them, but I pity them, just as I pity stage prompters and opera-glass manufacturers. I'm beginning to have a weak spot for the second and third best, from which the good always hides ever so slyly, if only from the fourth best—because to the audience it shows itself often. You can't blame it. The audience expects all that, the good has no choice. Or has it? Could it perhaps hide itself from the audience, showing its face instead to all the weaker possibilities? We'll have to wait and see. There are plenty of adequate rules in place—all those it takes so much to learn—and if I should chose to rely only on the inadequate ones, then that's my business.

I've also become weary of making connections. I don't say *while the rain pounds against the windows we are dragging the downfalls in front of us*, but I say *the rain which pounds against the windows* and *to drag the downfalls in front of yourself* and so forth. No one can force me to make connections as long as they are avoidable. I'm not indiscriminate the way life is—a better designation for which also just escaped me. Let's call it *life*, perhaps it doesn't deserve better. *Life* is not a special word and neither is *death*. Both are indefensible, they disguise instead of define. Perhaps I know why. Defining is close to undermining and it exposes you to the grip of dreams. But I don't really have to know that. I can stay out of it, I can very easily stay out of it. I can stand aside. Certainly I could mumble life and *living* to myself until I get sick of it, until I am forced to move on to another expression. Same with death, but I might have to mumble it even more often. But I don't. I restrain myself and I watch closely, this keeps me busy enough. I also listen closely, but listening entails certain dangers. One is easily overcome by ideas. Recently I heard *collect the downfall*, and it sounded like an imperative. I wouldn't want that. If it were a request, I might have considered it, but imperatives frighten me. That's why I moved to the second best. Because the best is always an imperative. That's why. Nothing will frighten me any more, I've had enough. And I've had enough of my thoughts, which in all honesty aren't my thoughts because if they were, they'd have a different name. Perhaps *my errors* but not *my thoughts.* They could be called anything, really. We've seen this often enough. Few things or people can defend themselves. They come into the world and immediately they are surrounded by all the things that will prove insufficient to contain them. Before they can even turn their heads they are confronted with designations—beginning with their own name—that will prove insufficient. Take lullabies, they provide many examples. Later it gets even worse. And I? I could defend myself. I could easily pursue the first best rather than just the best, but I don't. I don't want to stick out, I prefer to be indistinguishable. I watch closely. I watch closely how each and every thing is given its rushed and incorrect name—and lately I even join in. The difference is: I know what I'm doing. I know that the world is worse than its name, and that because of this, its name is also bad.

Collect the downfall. It sounds too good. Too sharp, too precise, too similar to the cries of late birds—a better name for pure truth than pure truth is. If I were to use this phrase I could possibly stick out, I could be lifted from my humble and hard-earned position in the ranks of namers and forever lose my observation post. And that I'd rather not. I'll stick with my rain pounding against the windows, in proximity to all the appropriated old wives' tales. And so if there have to be downfalls, then only those you drag in front of yourself. This last part seems almost too precise—perhaps we need to drop downfalls altogether. They are too close to what they stand for, like silent decoys circling around the norm. Norm is good—norm in any case is always inexact enough: norm and the pounding rain, all the first and all the last names, all of which will go on for ever while you remain the silent observer you'd like to be, watched approvingly from one direction or the other, keeping your hands in your pockets and leaving the downfalls unto themselves, or leaving them out, leaving them be—that's good. To leave be— that's almost too good in fact, absurdly good. No, away with the downfalls they only attract unwanted precision. Plus, they never occur in lullabies.

The rain which pounds against the windows, here it goes again, the rain, we'll leave it, rain keeps everything in its imprecise orbit, we'll stick with it so that *we* remains we, so that everything remains what it is not— from the weather to the angels.

This is one way to live and one way to die, and those who think this is not imprecise enough can keep experimenting along these lines. There will be no limits for them.

Stains

We now have stains on our armchairs. It looks like someone spilt sweetened milk. These stains have to be considered. Who spilt the milk, and when? Was it a guest and did he run away, a child perhaps? It could have easily been a child, though there are also adults who like to drink sweetened milk. And when? In the late morning or towards the evening? And would the world be different without these stains? This is a pointless question. It would be different. It would be without the stains. Of course the Rocky Mountains or the Catskills would still exist, hospitals with diphtheritic children and hopelessness of all kinds, or the pretty house in which Longfellow watched his pretty daughters grow up. But even all these things, which have long been integrated into the inventory of our desperate or cheerful souls, would be different. They would be without the stains on our armchairs. Not that they would wear their snow-covered heads, or whatever it is they have, any differently—but they would appear, for example, in a different sequence, because then the stains on our armchairs wouldn't have to be integrated in the hierarchy of our inventory, and now they have to be. And with the changing hierarchy the points of view from which we consider what ought to be considered also change.

But where is he who altered our world, the swift child or outlandish adult who caused the stains? Did he run away, did he sneak away? Did he panic and bang his head on the door frame, or did he walk away gracefully? Was he caught or not? Perhaps it was his last or second-to-last attempt to find consolation—probably the second-to-last. Sweetened milk. And then came the last one. Which could be called Dover—these journeys are common. But the stains, the sweetened-milk stains? They are not. They concern us. We can't include them in the sequence, giving the hierarchy one of those little nudges, which do no harm because they were part of the plan to begin with. Because such nudges belong to the changes that are provided for, like death—life's cunning manoeuvres for which room is reserved from the very beginning, though admittedly sometimes too little. That's the way it's supposed to be. Didn't you know that? Stop shivering. That's what it's like with journeys, or with death. But not with the stains on our armchairs. Journeys and deaths change the horizontal plane. There goes another, we say flippantly, and close the gap. But our stains change the vertical plane. The hierarchy begins to sway, but not out of fear. The hierarchy is not like a sufferer who can be glared at. It causes suffering. It is blind, deaf and always in danger of collapsing where you least expect it. Day is breaking, but the stains are still here.

Perhaps it will help to observe them. To behold them as the centre of all the explanations that never arrive. As a game that gave itself up before it even began, because it realized—against all expectations—that it wasn't meant to be a game, and that it was therefore all the more necessary to give itself up. Milk stains, even sweet ones—and giving yourself up is beginning to pay off. A way for you to cut back. Better yet: a way of cutting you back. Everything between heavens and hells, including heavens and hells—all these exclusive realms that make the mouth water, or burn. Nothing will be left, or rather: not nothing. Nothing that calls for attention. Better to never call for attention. But the vertical plane of appearances begin to sway. Something that wasn't provided for suddenly occurred—undercutting even the bare minimum. Take policemen, for example, they help each other, as do gods, or self-destroyers. But this milk—plus something else that doesn't fit into the picture, and in such a minimal amount? Spilt not on a table—this would be coherence—but on armchairs, on leather-like covers, probably imitation leather. Little cause for nausea. Not to be considered. In no way comparable to young, wild rivers, or to any immediate danger. If one could only call the stains drifters—but that's also impossible. The plural of a wipeable in-between existence which can't be constructed with words. So good, so far, far. Can't be discussed with anyone, can't be deciphered. There is a form of modesty that is unrelated to modesty, or even to immodesty. There are these unbearable forms, and they are spreading. But not very far. Because it would be impossible to rip open these gaps any further. Stains, stains! Their borders are demarcated by the state of dryness. At some point they must have been wet—perhaps just a moment ago. Now their former wet state exposes them to ridicule. But not in the middle of the whole sphere of ridiculousness, rather, towards the edge. No, not even the edge: towards a middle zone close to the edge. But there they are. Perhaps what counts in the end are only the ridiculous things—for this is where the secret heartbeats might begin. Was it not a child after all?

These children! One could take comfort in that. Children, only moments before they find their dead fathers, how carelessly they can step over a threshold, their gaze gliding over the walls, and the mug with the comforting beverage (and is there ever enough comfort, consolation) first in both hands, then in one hand only, then finally put down. At chair level. Right there. And then bumping it just once before they take again what's theirs and withdraw, step by step, with their backs towards the threshold, and then they cross it. Mirror images, a dance. Soon everything will be over, the various heights, the states of wetness, dryness, all states. No more time to wipe up what was spilt. No more time to look around. The dead fathers will win. The stains win, too. If only it really happened that way? But who can know this? The stains are teachable teachers. Don't try too hard to console yourself. The word in question was heights, not the highest. There's no way to know that this is how it happened. Anything could be imagined. It could have been a snail. No, no, quite certainly not a snail, and not a pikestaff either. But apart from these there are many possible ways to explain the origins of the stains. Perhaps such possibilities are the beginnings of all imagination. Because perhaps there are no beginnings. The stains win. They also win.

Doubts about Balconies

Balconies in the home countries are different. They are attached more securely, and you step out onto them more quickly. But caution is advised because the balconies in home countries are different. Because their construction allows for things that wouldn't be possible on other balconies. Because the way they are attached—even to the weakest walls, and no matter who attached them, a careless worker or a fearful one—is very different from the way that balconies are attached in foreign lands. It is identical to the perilous attachment of a loyalty that doesn't know itself. You step outside, the air caresses you fondly and you don't immediately notice it. You step outside again, and you still don't notice. The word xaíre might be written with shining letters above the balconies, or there might be only a bare wall—neither of which will change anything. The balconies will not be explained or understood by this. The way they are constructed is irrelevant, the shape of their railings even more so. They are the balconies of home countries and that alone indicates their position among the balconies of the rest of the world. A field might stretch out to the right—but what is a field for something that's only defined by itself? What do the balconies of home countries care about suburban streets, about filling stations or duck ponds? Old legends don't harm them; pear trees leave them indifferent. Various exegeses suggest that on Judgement Day they will be summoned separately and in all likelihood end up on the right, with the angels—they will find a way. It's not hard to imagine how the balconies will surge up to the angels, clutching each other, lovingly lifted by wings, and it's scary to think what could come of this, how they could use this to their advantage. Perhaps they would first change their names. *Heavenly Home Balconies* or *Balconies of the Eternal Home Country*. All this is unbearable to imagine. And how will they attach themselves? Are the many heavenly mansions made for this? Or will the balconies end up decorating, like giant wire toys, the eternal groves—clustered as they are, clutching each other? We must wait and see. In any case, they will land on the right, and they radiate their certainty about this so strongly that you can see it from afar. Even today, and even yesterday, and even the day before yesterday. The fact that they could be seen as foreign balconies—from somewhere else, from a foreign country—doesn't diminish their certainty. This view doesn't make any sense for them. And that's why they're dangerous. All the little tea parties, and all the lonely men who use the balconies on long early-summer afternoons—they don't suspect anything. No tea party will ever be able to tell who among them will, on Judgement Day, land on the right or the left, no man or woman knows this about themselves—but the balconies of home countries do. Their guilt can never be proven. Their merits are beyond question. Balcony, home country, view—and then always the retreat back into the room. Even though the balconies are immobile, they lull everyone who steps on them into a false sense of security. They transfer what can't be transferred, and they pass off the last days—including Judgement Day—as the first days, and perhaps they even greet whoever walks by with their insolent χαίρε. Insolent, that's what they are, they believe they have the monopoly on peace, yet they have never spent a dime on it, and they distract from thinking. And they always renew themselves everywhere. Farewells are exchanged on them, or discussions about crotchet patterns or deceptions. No one can harm them as long as what defines them exists: balconies and home countries. And both will exist for ever, there are forces appointed to see to that. 'Son!' the mothers shout in surprise and leap up from their outdoor chairs when their sons return from their military exercises and let their caps fall onto the balcony floors. 'Son, there you are, finally!' And here they are, on the balconies. Memories are exchanged. The balconies of home countries are small wind shelters. 'Do you remember how we played Halma here?' Yes, harmlessness that's it—the balconies have plenty of harmlessness in store, Halma and tea, and homework, and the soldiers' caps unnoticed on the floor. The mothers are pleased. This is partly due to the oxygen, the healthy fresh air— and the more rare this air becomes, the more the balconies of home countries will learn to use it to their advantage.

Not so with foreign balconies. Onto them you can only stumble—perhaps tripping over a threshold—and stare uneasily at the low railings and the foreign language ads of insurance companies on the opposite buildings, until a sudden gust of wind hits your face and you retreat, startled, back into the room as soon as politeness towards the unknown hosts allows it. It is quite impossible to imagine settling for an extended period of time on a foreign balcony. 'Foreign balconies' you think to yourself, and that's it. You didn't plan on bringing your wolfhound here, or expect that he would be allowed to sniff the strange railings, to rush onto the balcony past the legs of the foreign hosts, breathing the unfamiliar air with curiosity. You didn't expect anything. There are no disappointments on foreign balconies, this much is clear.

On the balconies of the home countries however, animals are the norm. They push past house plants and take their spot under balcony tables, even though on Judgement Day there will be no spot reserved for them, neither on the right nor the left. The balconies of the home countries are not bothered by this. They are uninterested. It goes unnoticed that this lack of interest equals deception. Who considers that a wolfhound under a balcony table in a home country might expect to go to heaven? Certainly the balconies of foreign countries are more honest. No animal resting on them will ever expect eternal bliss—unless of course it's a foreign animal. That's a different matter, for obvious reasons. Only outlandish lambs on outlandish balconies would fancy that some eternal pasture is reserved for them. And we know why. And certainly we have also, and for a long time now, begun to know too much, and also to think too much about peculiar things like the balconies of home countries. No one told us to do so. And thinking about the differences between foreign balconies and home balconies will lead to a fragmentation with unforeseeable outcome. Who could possibly—after having started on this path—innocently lean on the banister of a balcony ever again and let the rising sun or moon unfold their impressions on his soul?

The sun of home countries, the moon of home countries. This is going very far. It goes to show that the ability to differentiate should not be awakened unless it's already awake. And that this ability must never advance as far as balconies—they are certainly the limit. But can we ever go back? Can anyone who has recognized the balconies of home countries as the balconies of home countries ever reject this knowledge? Or simply preserve it in his heart? This is questionable. Nothing will ever reassure him, not even the definite demise of half-demolished balconies, or of all houses with balconies. He will live in uncertainty, he is in his home country.

'I love the beautiful village where I was born'— he learnt this in school. 'There my young life blossoms, close to my love's bosom, in an ever mirthful morn.' Later, unfortunately, the thought about balconies was added to this, the thought about the inscrutability of home balconies—and then his morning lost its mirth. Arbours might be acceptable but no, he isn't concerned with arbours here. He's concerned with balconies, and this weighs on him heavily, it darkens his mood. There are fewer and fewer things he can discuss with friends. At first they only laughed, or became thoughtful, but at least for a few afternoons they debated the issue with him. Then they grew impatient. And now he's alone with his balconies, with his desperate knowledge, his razor-sharp differentiations which give him no peace of mind. When did this begin, when did it first occur to him?

The balconies of the home countries. 'Inapplicable,' someone replied. He can't stop thinking about this word. Aren't balconies more or less an application? To be applied in order to better consider what a home country is? And can applications be inapplicable? No, no, he's right—but this rightness makes him lonely. 'In truth you're talking about yourself,' another person said. Himself? God forbid. What does he have in common with balconies? That person went too far, but that's how far they are willing to go. He will no longer confide in anyone. He is not a balcony, that much is certain—and surely he is not the balcony of a home country. He is inaccessible, and he doesn't count on landing on the right, where the angels are, when Judgement Day dawns. And he doesn't deceive animals, he considers them. He is not the kind of person you can just walk all over because you think you have the right to do so, and who would accept it like an angel. He has faults, but not these: he doesn't offer deceptive views. Legends and pear trees don't leave him indifferent. Paths and directions are not irrelevant to him. He is different from the balconies of home countries. He is not content.

But what if he were? He himself the balcony of a home country in a home country? He will travel to evade this question, he will go far away. One day perhaps you will see him again—but not this way, he will make certain of it. He will pursue his unhappiness far into the distance, where it belongs. No, he himself is not a home balcony. But who is, and who are they, the balconies of home countries, these huge, inconspicuous deceivers? Should he let them be, should he simply let them go on deceiving? At the very least they only deceive the ones who want to be deceived. Or who shall be deceived. He will continue to ponder this question, he will search the heavens. He will get the idea, but he will never get *in*. He will never conspire with the balconies of home countries. So what if they take over the angel's wings, the celestial walls, the eternal home countries. He won't be there when it happens.

The Connoisseurs of Western Columns

The snow on the capitals of Western columns is only unbearable for outsiders. The small outsiders—those who we'd like to leave behind anyway, those who prevent progress. Better to stay on the side of the encadred ones, since the snow on the capitals leaves them colder than it already is. The snow. It's not cold enough. If it were colder the snow would preserve the form of the Western columns, it would stabilize them, enclose them for ever, and it wouldn't recede even under the weakest sun. Yet the way it is now the snow only produces fissures, accelerating the downfalls which don't bother those who've been encadred but only, once again, the outsiders, who invented the beginning of unbearableness. Helplessly the outsiders circle the columns while the others bypass them, and look gleefully at the battlefields further below that are now planted with oats, shouting the battlefields' melodic names to one another, or rubbing their hands or patting each other on the shoulder—depending on the temperature—while the outsiders, the bewildered ones, stay where they are, paying little attention to the oat fields below. They know the oats, they know they will blossom soon. The oats do not blossom for them, and that's why they know them. Pretty oats. Do they in fact blossom? Straw doesn't blossom. They turn away. One by one they go back to their old places. There are good people among them. Painters who have almost run out of yellow, structural planners for small stables who have a mind of their own, tinsmiths, private folks, opponents of hunting, all kinds of people. The only thing they all have in common is that the Western columns are on their minds, the old cracked Western columns, and the flat hill—and that the snow wouldn't bother them if it didn't also fall on the Western columns. The others however—let's simply call them the encadred—are bothered by snow in general, though they often claim the opposite, yet on the Western columns, it doesn't bother them. These are the differences, we admit they are slight but they can't be explained away. And that's why people try to suppress them, and that's why people don't bother if the painter with his diminished paint turns around, or the plumbers and the hunting opponents and all the others, too. You can safely let them be, they won't conspire. Soon enough, the painter will run out of yellow then red; the tinsmiths will run out of nails then tin; and the private folks and the hunting opponents, well, they have long run out of most things anyway. No, there's no need to worry about these kinds of people, their enthusiasm for Western columns speaks for itself. Any bounty on their heads would be a waste. Best to leave them alone. They die, too, whereas the others only sing 'Dying is necessary,' and then they lie down to sleep, but not for long. Those who don't sing but simply die don't even need to be classified anywhere— Connoisseurs of Western Columns is a decent collective designation, and it won't survive for very long, at which point everything will be in order again: the view on the battlefields which are sufficiently cultivated with oats, and on the gentle downward paths, and also on other paths that, significantly, always lead into the background, to the dwellings of the bewildered ones and the non-singers. All those paths will no longer be disturbed by a few scattered, darkened and possibly crouched figures. Their paint boxes will dry out, and their shabby tin scraps will rust, and the hunting opposition will fall silent. Because they don't sing—for ever. Mould will grow in their barren rooms. Their doubtful, often painful, often wild glances at the snow on the Western columns will become unnecessary; their careful and fearful steps around the plinths will end and leave no trace. One must simply have a grain of patience, one must only wait a while longer, and everything will be in order again.

In the meantime, though it might be necessary to be alert, and to observe the Connoisseurs unobtrusively, and to make sure that they remain isolated. Not a difficult task, especially if you divide it up, organize yourself in groups, and proceed in an orderly way. Just to be sure. Certainly this could be achieved more quickly by simply bringing down the already crumbling Western columns and letting them roll into the oat fields; but it won't be necessary. Once the oats begin to grow, to bloom and stand tall, the Connoisseurs of Western Columns will probably already lie in the ground underneath, mingled with the poor dishonoured remains of those who involuntarily participated in the battles. (The others lie somewhere else, their memory celebrated in the well-known song.) And Western columns without the Connoisseurs of Western Columns are harmless. They don't prop up anything but the sky, and the sky has long been supporting itself. The columns are but memory props without memory, they obstruct road construction and could easily fall on playing children. Which would rub the others, the encadred, the wrong way. Because the encadred ones show that they care deeply about youth, and therefore also about road construction, about the accurate division of the land. Of course, the old battlefields would be spared; they are already farmed, and they loosen up the landscape. They are a reminder of something—and the things they remind us of are by now secured knowledge. Fields don't poke up into the air but instead lie flat, in plain view, integrated into the normalized compartments of memory. Fields wouldn't be harmed if something suddenly fell from the sky, only the oats would be harmed, but only in years with bad forecasts. However, the Western columns are harmed by everything, starting with the ridiculous snow, the harmless snow, the snow made for children's hearts. Harmful also is the spring rain, or the summer heat which helps yield the fruit of the earth. Couldn't one say, and with good conscience, that they are vermin—since the useful and unwavering rhythms of nature harm them? And vermin, also, are those that cling to them.

Western columns. Why weren't they built under a different sky, under a sky without the power to crush what they once held up, and to leave them standing like useless crutches, crumbling? They don't even form a natural border, like rivers sometimes do, they just stand there, defined only by the spaces between them, which are useless. They must have been brought forth by a kind of idiocy—a thought that's hard to bear for the cheerful among those whose ancestors inhabited these lands. So can you blame them for forming cadres, for wanting to take action in whatever way possible?

The Connoisseurs of Western Columns will then become the Defenders of the Western Columns, and it's downhill from here on. They are used to downhills, but downhills have a natural limit. After they have reached a certain point, one can safely call them downfalls. For the time being though, one might be content with small downhills, one follows after the other—demise, that's also a good word. The Connoisseurs are obstinate and this harms them, their isolation harms them, their limping gait, one of every two drags his feet behind. They are even incapable of joining, sharing or discussing their mutual love for the seven columns. Sowhy not let them come and sand down the capitals with their fearful eyes, the snow on top, the cracks that fork down. Why not let them, for a short time, safely circle the columns, circle everything that will eventually fall? For the Connoisseurs of Western Columns are lost.

The Guest

Adolphe visits his aunts twice a year. There are people who think he visits them twice a week, but that's an outlandish thought. He visits them twice a year. However, he always pretends that he visits them almost daily. He takes the key to their gate, which he often carries with him, and he goes there right after school, he crosses the front yard, quickly jumps up the four or five low steps, unlocks the door and—there he is. He seldom brings flowers and if he does, only violet ones, a sparse bouquet for both of them. This probably happens every one and a half years. More rarely he brings boutonnieres. He doesn't mind visiting them. In the hallway—which appears to be darker than necessary due to the variously coloured windows—he calls them with a loud voice. He hugs them and tells them the news of the morning. His stories never go further back into the past. He says, Mr Meyers has a cold. When he talked about Stoics in third period he could barely breathe. It was like this—. And he imitates Mr Meyers who has a cold. Or he says, Anne wrote from

Penzance. I'm curious how long she'll hold out in that hamlet. The letter was stuck in the door this morning. Anne is his sister. Then he says again, The Stoics are hard to memorize. They're not for me. Adolphe is not a bad entertainer. Every now and then he takes off his glasses and wipes them clean, he tastes and admires the tea. He listens to questions. He says he can very well imagine that one is plagued by headaches, mostly one-sided ones, particularly today. Yes, with the way the air was today, and in the classrooms, too. Surely there's no connection to the damp fur coats hanging in the hall-way, nor the fact that the house faces north-east. In the afternoon, he will study the Epicureans, he thinks they are more accessible and perhaps they could even help him memorize the Stoics. In this way, he introduces the afternoon into the conversation. It always seemed to him, he says, that the afternoon was a kind of doubt about the afternoon, whereas the morning was a kind of belief in the morning. Today it was the same thing. As one can see, he takes his aunts seriously enough to place certain demands on their conversation. But he never takes his demands too far. Stoa, he suddenly says, lengthening the 'a', and laughs. He wonders how Anne is doing in Penzance, he says, particularly with regard to mornings and afternoons. Anne is blonde and that changes quite a few things, ideas and conceptions might turn into their opposites. And then Penzance is really far out west. He smiles, and looks at the north-eastern bay windows. No, the west should never be taken too far, not even for the sake of the afternoon sun. Anne will certainly come back. Of course, that's what he assumes. Penzance is simply an exaggeration. It is exaggerated, certainly. Adolphe makes his words sound final, but as if not to frighten the aunts, or to worry them with the thought of an overly sudden departure, he leans back and unbuttons two buttons on his vest. And soon enough he starts to talk about his fondness for vests, single-coloured, multi-coloured, bright ones and dark ones. He has a collection of them. And he takes care of them. With a decent vest, one could even dare walk barefoot, he says. Of course that would be uncomfortable. For a moment, Adolphe falls silent. He knows better than to go too far with this topic. He even says so. Every topic has its risks, he says. Haven't they also experienced this? He's actually curious. One can also have experiences without regarding them as experiences. Perhaps that's a more efficient way of having an experience. In the end this helps philosophers, and then one must study them at school. The abridged versions. The commentators. Mr Meyers.

Adolphe is getting a bit uneasy. It seems he hasn't been swift enough in evading the risks that come with every topic. He takes more tea. He begins to praise the colours of the window frames. Flaking or not, he says, they fit nicely. And surely many window frames in the world can appear oppressive and cold, can't they? He noted this on his tours of ships—Anne too, back when she was still here. Now of course Anne has been gone for a long time and who knows what kind of window frames she sees in Penzance. Yes, that's it. Not that Anne wouldn't make a good picture in any frame, that's not the point. Adolphe begins to cough, he thanks the aunts politely for their help, he drinks some water, he's coughing harder now, he takes a piece of sugar and thanks them again. But now he looks angry. He suddenly jumps up and walks over to the window, where he leans lightly on the windowsill and looks outside. It is obvious that he is looking out intensely. Ridiculous, this cough, he says, and turns back into the room, but not to worry, something can be found to treat it. He simply mustn't speak of boats, or of museum tours of boats, perhaps he should avoid Penzance altogether. And surely, he has useful cough drops at home, also calming in general. Adolphe is now composed once again. Menthol, he says, best of all with milk. Can you imagine, he asks, milk with menthol? This idea seems to calm him down, he appears more forgiving now. He smiles. He sits down again and remarks that girls nowadays are often called Melissa, such as the newborn sister of a friend. One tiny little Melissa after another. For boys such a clear preference has yet to be seen. This seems to be a topic worth studying. These waves from name to name. With priorities or without priorities. And of all things—Melissa. People really don't rack their brains enough about the names they choose. But it could be revealing, couldn't it, and protect one from harm. Sometimes one is overcome by foolish fears, he says. What if all this business of naming, all this imbalance, would simply disappear? Improbable from the viewpoint of statisticians, but still highly likely. Like carnival guilds. Before the founding of carnival guilds, one should have asked a statistician if there was any probability that they could be founded, if there existed any discourse that would argue both for the thing itself, and for its name. And both in one. What do they think he'd have said? There is none, he'd have replied. Adolphe himself, no, he's certainly not planning on becoming a statistician. To be more precise: he has banned this possibility from his mind, though he's aware of the fact that his mind

could change unexpectedly. Towards statistics. Growth
or austerity or atrophy, says Adolphe, it's very easy to
solicit agreement with such possibilities, same with the
confessed or unconfessed love for the big picture.
Adolphe is laughing now, as if this love was improbable
to him. He laughs reluctantly, a kind of overhasty laugh
and yes, he's in a hurry. He doesn't like to be in a hurry,
it's clearly against his nature. Adolphe always wants to
be sketched and he knows that being in a hurry and
smiling could harm the sketched portrait. Adolphe has
his own ideas about sketched portraits but he doesn't
think that they're only his ideas. He once saw a sketch
of someone blowing out a candle. It was a failure.
Anyone who extinguishes lights must be in a hurry—
a big hurry. Blind zeal always correlates with the zeal
to go blind. Adolphe knows that it doesn't suit him to
be in a hurry. Some fine day, here at his aunts' house,
he will meet the one who will capture him. Someone
who can't stop teasing him while observing him—
Adolphe, with his legs stretched out, or smiling at the
window. Talking about Mr Meyers and philosophy.
About Melissian names and milk with menthol.
And so forth and so forth. All this would have to be
visible in the sketch. A squint that doesn't need itself.
All the possible aspirations, but not the people who

are tormented by those aspirations. Not those who have been ruled out to begin with. No benefactors, not even at the very bottom, not even hidden under the frame as soon as it's framed. Yes, indeed, that's how it should be. And as it will be. Adolphe suddenly feels tired, he stifles a yawn. He wants to talk again about Anne and Penzance, but he won't. His sister Anne must stay out of the game when the game gets tired. He is angry. It has always been like that. It is always like that. It is always the thought about his own image that initiates the beginning of the end. The thought about a few pencil scribbles that are supposed to live up to him. He now takes a cordial. And one more. He revels in the desperate taste that will drive him away, that masks his morning stories and his afternoon stories, too. The good tea. He bids his aunts farewell. He doesn't say that he will come back, he never does. He says, however, while eager to hide his haste, that he hopes they will have a pleasant afternoon. Surely in the garden or perhaps better inside. He sincerely hopes he didn't stay too long. But the window frames he can't praise enough, no really, he can't. He wishes he'd find such window frames everywhere he goes. They really are a lifesaver. They could protect you from anything. He laughs. Indeed. Underrated things in any case are a topic. He will try to include them in his classes at school. As inconspicuously as possible, of course. He laughs again. Didn't he forget something? No, of course not, there were only the flowers he brought, and they will stay here. He says it's the same every time. Almost every time he thinks he forgot what he brought. He's impossible. And he laughs again. He can feel free to laugh now, distorted and chuckling and grimacing. The one who was supposed to capture him, that scribbler, he didn't come. And he won't come any more. Again it was all for nothing.

Ambros

Ambros climbs under the steps. Tries to repair the steps with a hammer because one step was loose. He hammers with his face turned up, and there's no friend in sight to disturb him, or to ask where he's from and where he intends to go. All his friends have gone under the earth, there is said to be some kind of party there, but he didn't go. It's a humid day. So far only one of his friends has come back from down below. He passed by and—shooting a glance over the fence—said it wasn't worth it in the end, only at the beginning. And to go down under the earth only for a beginning is pretty much pointless, he says, because coming up is even more tedious then going down. Pointless as any beginning, now that he thinks about it—this much he shouted, and walked away quickly. Now that I think about it, thinks Ambros. This much and no more. Now that I really think about it. And once again. But no more. Now that he actually thinks about it. Ambros, three nails between his teeth, keeps hammering. At times it sounds as if he were pounding on the earth.

On the thing everyone is talking about. Or the thing under which they are now talking. In one manner or another—it's always one. Always the one he tries to understand if he doesn't understand it—and tries not to understand if he has understood it. Like their dances below. Bordering on violence. Don't be bullied, one of them said, but which one? A person who remembers nothing always has a choice. And a person who has a choice is a good person, he loves no more. Loves no one more than another, and thus he's a fair man. But who says he is fair? Someone should just go ahead and try. One of those upright people, those who have fuses between their teeth. Is no one else coming back from the party? It really should be over soon. Equals seven times five. Equals three plus the ascent. The Ascension. Coming back again. The ride is not free for the likes of you, what were you thinking, guys —the way you burden earth with cigarette butts, and put pressure on it all the time, in every possible way. You with your ape weights! Yes, I mean you. And you. You, too. Oh, and now you act surprised. It's closing time in these quarters, nothing more can be done. Perhaps they just thought they could stay and keep sitting here. Some thinkers they'd be, oh yeah, some fine thinkers they are. And where did you leave the little one who was with you the other day? Oh, he won't come back? He had enough of you, huh, and what is he doing now? He's hammering? Yes, he's hammering, up there. He's fine, the little one. Let him hammer. And when he gets tired, where will he lie down? In his own staircase, under those steps, just like sons in fairy tales? Ambros wants to break out of the staircase, the front yard, the front lawn, he wants to run past his mother and father and towards the ones who will soon be silenced. He wants to shout: Come! Everyone come at once, pull your heads out of the sand, call my name, all together! He knows that they will—that they will come. The party will need to end because it is not a party after all. He wants to tell them: It's only a whim they've fallen for. He wants to summon them as if they were lions and savages: Come. Don't let anyone weaken your cries, you know that's not who you are. The little friendly guy with the zebra-striped hat: that's not me, and it's not any of you either. None of the benches down here were ever made for you. They are material benches, and material tables, and the wine, too, is only meant for the material—same with the floors, the walls, the doors, the ceilings, the windows and windowsills. So that the material can gaze outside, so that its gaze reflects properly back on itself, all the way through, and so that none of you notice that everything is upside down: all the earthy free-range and open air down there, the fake light, the beer gardens with their upward ducts. Don't let them trick you, don't abandon your desires!

Up here everything is different. Here everything flashes, silvery and white, and you no longer need to take the nails from your teeth when you speak, not for any sound, any syllable you prefer not to speak. Here you are released, and you can hammer on steps like I do, or you can do anything you want, anything with nails. This will do you good. The heavens, up here, are real—they have nothing in common with the shirred and sheared wool from down there. Don't get involved, the nails are very good. And that's all I have to say.

Will they come? Will they not be lured by the fresh meadows below, by their insincere blend of colours, their feigned blooming? Won't they surrender to all the entertainment that the bartenders provide? And what about all the pennies necessary for the ascension? These are the questions. Ambros. And what will the next one be called? Will the naming proceed according to notes, semiquavers, crotchets, quavers, according to the measure of four, or what? What system will they follow? Do they hear him hammering?

He wants to make earthly sounds because nothing sounds like wood any more, so wild and silent. He wants to make signs. Never give away anything—do you hear me, down there—keep everything to yourselves. But the steps will soon be repaired. Soon his parents' house will be finished, and he will no longer be able to produce sounds. When everything is fixed, he will no longer be heard. There will be no smoke, no rustling, no clattering, no hammering.

Dover

Werld would be better than world. Less useful, less apt. Orth better than earth. But this is the way it is now. Normandy is called Normandy and not anything else. Same goes for the rest. Everything is attuned. To each other, as one says. And as one sees. And as one doesn't see, either. Only Dover is impossible to improve. Dover is called exactly what it is. All the names and what they designate are easily unhinged from this place of (as many people think) little importance. Delft, Hindustan, also *beyond*. Even though *beyond* is not a place. Or most likely not. But Dover, persistent and close to the edge, doesn't use its power. That is its unique quality. Whoever embarks or disembarks in Dover only looks around briefly, and doesn't notice anything. Dover, incorruptible and quiet between the pitfalls and inaccuracies, doesn't call attention to itself. Chalk cliffs and one or two lullabies from one or two wars: you can't be more modest than that. To perish in Dover is almost as easy as perishing in Calcutta, with its pestilence and its oddly chosen name, its hot smoke. In Dover, one can learn how to walk hunched over, or learn how to rage, or learn how to hop—same as anywhere else. But only because of Dover will all these things remain utterly clear to the one who learns them. He can later move away, he can go on to operate merry-go-rounds, or to furnish offices, but what he picked up in Dover he will never lose, and what he became in Dover—a hunchback, a madman, a clown—will make him invincible. Annie, for example, moved away at an early age and all she learnt in Dover was how to drool. But she was still skilled at it in Denver, where she landed in a madhouse at age ninety, and she was skilled at it to such a degree that the nurses shivered with envy and angry admiration whenever they moved Annie from one bed to another. And even while they shivered, they noticed that their shivering only corresponded to its drab designation, and not to what it really was. None of them had learnt it in Dover. But at the very least this gave them an inkling. And this is how Dover distributes precise inklings. Neither the air nor the water can hinder Dover, much less the earth. Much less its own chalk. Dover can respond to moods without being harmed by them. It can respond to little white cribs, with Johnnys in them, or red-cheeked Marys, or Dawns, or Deans. And to everything that is

117

designed to go *beyond*. And even to colours in general, however few exist. But Dover doesn't promote colour theory, it doesn't promote knowledge. The nurses in Denver will never learn what made them shiver. The few sailors who run aground in Dover don't understand, when they get stranded the next time in more distant, more likely places, why they deserve the frantic admiration of their comrades.

Anyone who would like, on a dull Sunday, to chat with Marlowe, or step on Wilde's lyre, or to make a life-size sketch of a house in Tudor-style, should simply focus on Dover. He will not meet Marlowe there, he will not find Wilde's lyre, and he will soon consider Tudor-style irrelevant. Instead, he will quickly and precisely sum up his wishes, and then he will want to play with pebbles. He will build a pebble playground high up near the cliffs. It will take a while, but he will learn how to play with pebbles like no one else can, how to handle them with fingers and feet, how to tame them. He will become a world-famous pebble player. He will become invincible even before Annie in Denver. We might say Dover has put his desires right where they belong. Or that Dover put them to rest. Pebble to pebble. Just look at him, high up there, bending down to the pebbles, gentle as no other. He must be right.

Besides, everybody knows that chalk stores are the way to learn about the world. This is said as an aside, but even speaking aside needs to be learnt. And whoever has not learnt it in Dover will have a hard time ever learning it. Despite all efforts he will relapse time and again into the main things—and this will depress him. And then he will meet the person who was asked to give a speech about King Arthur's roundtable at the cliff school in Dover, the one who failed at it, who was never asked again and thus started to speak in asides. About interstices, about hat strings, uninteresting stuff. This person will defeat him for good. But at the very least they inspire each other. Dover stays in the game.

If not for Dover, why would we ever examine our moments in time? Why do we value them highly, or not at all; why do we let someone steal them, or not? And how? How does one survive a moment that is still ahead in time but already lost, once and for all? Never mind the moments we supposedly gained, the ones that now lie behind, once and for all. How do we unlearn the ways of saying *recently* and *later, just now* and *soon*? Where, if not here? Everything happens in Dover. Dover knows the variety of disciplines which serve the moments. Entire university departments sprout in the swirling air above the cliffs, swaying—

with front entrances and rear entrances, with towers and low buildings, with camps and niches and escape plans. You can send your dreams to school here, and after they've graduated you can safely let them drown in the freshly dug wells which are here solely for this purpose. In Dover, everyone knows that the only thing that is ever under attack is the moment. In Dover, the correlation between walking bent over, walking upright, and walking away is always perfectly clear. Do you need to hear more?

No, no, we don't want this to be a third lullaby about Dover.

Lullabies always led to the hecatombs, and Dover simply omits hecatombs. It relies on lesser amounts, on the least amounts, on quick deprecations.

And what about friendships made in Dover? Do they survive, or do they dissolve once they're up against the familiar commensurabilities? It's either this way or that. Dover doesn't rely on friendships. Dover has its droolers, its rope-jumpers and pebble-players and its seldom-stranded sailors. It's either this way or that with friendships in Dover, you get what you get. And if it's this way or that, and if that's what you get, then Dover will always plead for us: whether in

Denver, in Trouville, or in Bilbao. It will entreat the places of the world for us with its easy gaze. It will keep an eye on the madhouse of Privas and all the other madhouses, too. It will not omit the things that don't measure up to it—it will draw on their weaknesses, and on its own weakness. It won't forget about industry, diligence, naivety, nor that everything will be over soon. It will not shove aside our failed desperation, which is all we have. Not Dover.

Privas

Privas is a headlock, an institution for rabid darlings, starting perhaps from the age of four. Don't get too close, dear Fräulein, to the tame little ones and the sweet foam at their mouths. You're not from here, so you'd be better off visiting the trade school and its current exhibitions—weaving tools, flying tools, duplicate walking tools. The exhibitions there change almost like far-off, persistent lightning, and there's always a doorman, a barrier to protect you from rabies, unless of course you've already caught it. In which case that would be entirely your fault. It would mean you'd probably tickled one of the mad little ones around her foamy mouth, and that you spent your insufficient pity on the wrong ones, the lost ones. You seem to have forgotten the most simple things, Fräulein, and that's really too bad. The current exhibition about crutches is very nice, hand-carved crutches, and upstairs the embroidery tools, all the net-mending methods with informative examples—all this would have been just right for you, but you can't come in, can you, because you've got the whole rabid bunch clinging to the hem of your dress. Had you come earlier, I could have explained to you: you help the ones who can be helped. And whoever cannot be helped will not be helped. The least you could do is to shoo the little beasts out of the hallway and away from the coat racks. Nothing will ever become of them, Fräulein, their future can easily be read from the coat racks covered in their sticky foam, it's stuck. It sticks to them, ha ha. But we'll sort it out with a bucket of suds. We'll wash it away. Once you're away. Can't you hurry up a little? We're used to everything here being a little hurrieder than elsewhere. That's of course why we're here. Here in Privas. Well good, you're finally stirring. But no, not like that, you're getting all tangled, and look, by now even your pleats have gone rabid. That means you'll simply have to learn to live with the pack—different moves, smarter manoeuvres. You have only yourself to thank.

And what gave you the idea? Privas is certainly unusual. And moreover on a day when the guard left open the gate to the rabies institution. What was it, the lack of choice, the wrong section on your small map, or a lost brother? What drove you to come here with your children's wagon? Perhaps you are a duchess, and you have demands. One never knows. After you've exited, after you've turned through the door with your damned pack, I recommend that you climb the cone-shaped hill with the jamming transmitter. A hot trail runs up the hill. The more delicate among your little yelpers will probably run out of foam early on. And the stronger ones, the outlandish ones that always howl 'why', will eventually be defeated by the jamming stations, because they tick. And once you're on the very top, alone, with your needlework basket, with no more than two cadavers hanging from your pretty patterned skirt, you'll finally look down at Privas. How it lies there, plucked and puffed out, gutted and dammed up. Not the stud farms, not the other animal-processing plants, and not the chestnut collection-points with which it prides itself. Privas, simply Privas. Where does it come from? Who chased it here? And who left it lying here for good with its insufficiently pleasant or unpleasant relationships to everything else? With its premature tall tales and its belated truths? Is there no cart anywhere to haul it further? Or is this what your little wagon was meant for, Fräulein? But you'd have to go very far away for Privas to become small enough to be picked up. Perhaps the cone-shaped hill will be just right. Perhaps from the very top it can be done with plenty of crochet yarn and once you've cut all the mad yappers from your skirt. Then you'll load Privas onto your darling little cart and haul it down the other side, which also has jamming stations, by the way. And you'll sing. You'll be carrying Privas on your cart, and that's what you wanted, right? Privas and nothing else, I can tell by looking at you, you hide it poorly, your ears are burning. On your cart they'll all be rattling: the vocational institutions and the chestnuts, and where will you bring them, Fräulein? It's windy today.

Perhaps to the coast, where the wind will quickly blow it off your cart. Or to the charred grounds way up high, where no one can ever dive to find it. But whether you clatter off to the country or off to the coast, you'll know where to go, you of all people will certainly know. Oh you and the tears you're shedding over the lost little yelpers, I know the likes of you. You made a vow that whatever happened in the past is always just about to happen, didn't you? You and your vows, Fräulein. For the likes of you, no map can ever be small enough to serve the purpose—all the maps of charred grounds and all the maps of drownings, all the hellish laughter. Privas will vanish because it's precious to you, and nobody knows why. You won't spit it out. On your cart, the teachers of the vocational institutions will be flustered from the thundering chestnuts, and that doesn't worry you? The whole idea? The cattle that will be spilt by the wayside, that no one can roast any more, the unused cowhides? There's milk dripping from your cart, my dear, and you don't even mind. The milk of Privas. But milk was never an issue for you, you never cared about Privas milk, or did you?

The only thing I'd like to know is what you will sing on your way, on the shorter or the longer part of the way that's still ahead of you and Privas. For you must be singing something. The teachers on your cart will have stopped shaking, and all the doormen, fence keepers and sheep-paddock leasers of Privas will have fallen silent, too. Now it's up to you. I can picture you quite well: frail and bony, frayed crochet yarn around your middle. Perhaps you only whistle. But I can't think of the song. 'Frère Jacques' would be a bad fit, and the song about the little Scotsman doesn't fit at all. But you'll think of something.

By then, the cone-shaped hill with the jamming stations will lie far behind you, and the foam on your skirt will have dried. No one will envy you for having Privas on your cart. All the pretty pieces in the trade museum will be broken and jumbled, the crutches stuck in the embroidery frames, chestnuts everywhere. Nothing that's worth giving away. Privas is all yours now, and the coasts are near, and so are the charred grounds. But how will you do it? Will you simply push the cart, or will you jump with it? Will you untie yourself from Privas, or not? I'm only asking, you don't have to say a word, you don't have to answer me. You can't.

Albany

Raving mad—oh how this ends, the end is a meadow, all these are meadows, pulled from dressers and rolled up into a bundle again, mind the edges of the bills, mine, mind, don't get too near, don't even appear—oh my, no nine, oh no, there were eight when we appeared, and the many heavy valises, valeurs, everything so fast, yes, yes, yes, yes, a canon was advertised, I remember that, on the switchboards, I remember that too, or it was advertised with the bus fares, I remember that too, me too, no—me, me too, and a young woman poured a bowl of octopi over us, over me too, and they all stuck to me, to the arms of my coat, they stuck to them, and all this not without intention: luckily she kept the bowl in her two hands, otherwise—what a mess.

Right. And then we moved on, here we are, here was that, that was that, that was what I said and nothing without intention, just like nothing itself, all without never—and Tina was supposed to scratch my back but she didn't, she did not, no one else either, of course not and no one again, no one as I say, I said it, yes, very good, didn't I say it and this is why we stay, this is why we are all in, through this, through this here; and then we all had to get jaundice, too, as if it wasn't bad enough, only Auguste didn't get it, differently and in general, she didn't get it, but we, we all did, except her of course, she, except of course she would have, would have had, had, had it—but no. She didn't get it, how this looked, there were train connections to all kinds of places, and modes of expressions, and a lottery ticket on the bare loam; there were masts, masks, no: masts, masses of, the mast, and lottery tickets to feed to the pigs, to feast—and I wanted to ask, how are they doing over there, how are those Quaker places, no I mean those, not the other ones, but the other wants, or otherwise—likewise with martini, nice to see, sir, or father, or pretty, but how do we do, we'll divide up the suitcase among us, then there's the road, all the same, the thirty-seventh time, last hockey, my brother Georg won three frontrunners and he also won in general, and Mother will bake you some iced celery, the jelly, and the jelly chapel must be finished by now, already and already, mind the water levels, there are big water levels here, they are growing—now we've been circling for an endless while, but how are things over there, I just can't imagine, no, no, not I, certainly not I—can't defend yourself when the sun goes awry, right, and Georg is in the army now. But Hermann —they doubted his good behaviour and progress, and the boxes with spices, too heavy for the boy, he should settle somewhere with his astronomy, that would be best for him, because he was never very strong, and now we've arrived at the question of style, or pneumatic tubes—other, or maybe not, leave her be, if you don't want this, not her.

He invented mast bees, he was the smaller one, but the bees stay away now, they tumble left and right out of your way and go astray, they leap up the cables, luckily the laggings, really, they dash up and *paff* on the hat— they were all gone and now they're back, they hold on tight and *plitz*, before you know it—Hermann was always funny and funny he never was, now he's ready, he will surely come, that too, but not all of them, he will even climb up without a mast, he is more level-headed than the taller one, more attuned, he'll notice us right away, the mast bees for sure, the remaining question and all that, people make things easier for themselves when it comes to the umpteenth time, so it is, that, that is how it is, ideas, ideas and that's also what one says.

Tina didn't have it bad, shall we say, *total*, that's what it means, the girls have a certain way about them, Auguste too, but we, not we, we're not away, we're all here—we were put on this course and we move quickly, but who, who did this, who brought the old chest this far, who broke it, this I'd like to know, who? The holes between the masts and the wings, who was it, he should report it, and report himself as well, and then it's simple, please come to the blackboard, my boy, prove that square roots are juicy, that they can be squared or cubed, that one can extract them from familiar meadows, you simply pull and pull and there, there, in next to no, or 20 miles from the centre, we won't trade this, no, no, we'll stick to our ansatz, on our praised spot of land, where father extracts carrots, and your mother dries them over the drain, and when you're finished you can drive to city hall and collect your share—Auguste, if she's the first, then she will be the first, or if it's Tina, then it's Tina, it was always like—the footpath is historical and the road is also, it was always like this, on the dot, and a discount is only granted if a half hour is full, at every full half—now picture this—if your courage will let you, if your fresh senses will let you, sifted and double, and dispensed by the dear heavens, by this very one, by mine, me, yours, this goes and smooth and it goes, this was easy to grasp now, wasn't it.

But what now? Totally warped, one could say, wovenly so, but we are staying, hey, here, here, here, it sounds as if it was over and gone, or off and gone, or gone off, or over gone—but we will stay. We clasp our hooks, and the cookie helps us to go home, it rolls us and it bodes us well, it strays us in so that no grain shall spill, it flattens and it is smooth, it is called thus, it became, and then the thing with the snack shops, sure, this works, but not any other way, bracketed by the big figures, and this ought to be, they are big, they are really big and they all found each other, none's missing, and quiet, for to admire, admire quickly such a little eleven, eleventh, or elver, or elwer—Elwer was a quiet one, an immigrant, clearly, but no one notices, he leans casually on the cattle fence, he is our guard, how does he find the morning, how do you find the morning, sir, not yet, how dost thou find the morning, he, the morning, Your Honour, the rascal watches us, and there's no breakfast tea, no burnt *brode*, no breader, no warranty.

The others behave similarly, perhaps they want to become guides, city guides, or municipal-building couriers, meadow developers, or female developers, how about a thousand, no, you have no choice, in the end they will easily find their way, stick to the even numbers and the straight lines, they are straight fellows, and who would not root for them as long as they would root for him, and who wouldn't treat them right, and hold in sight what they scream into his ear, gods and god-fearing, good boys.

The morning calls us to our walks, it calls and it is called and it is called morning until it's over, walked-over and gone, and it easily got out of a tight spot, or spots, or pots, a watched pot—everything is there, the good morning, and how easily it trumpets across the land, such woe and such woundedness, so much woundedness until here, and so hard to foresee, and this trend seems to stay, you can't stop it with lamp tricks or such things, it won't work, it will stay, it will take—yes, take the dog with you, on your grandfather's side, the line ends there, intense and noble and not to be deflected, and the dog will get nothing, he will be trimmed, and kept in line, barren morning, yes, barren, he didn't get anything, perhaps a few bottlenecks, or needle eyes, easy to wander through, accessible, to draw through the eye of, needles, to be drafted through, those especially, the route is free and fluctuates on every level, on camp grounds, a route like a horse's hair, but the hair taken from a foal, deduced from or derived from, and now run, my little horse, run like it's normal, let's run now and deflect in the end, swinging or winged, says the statue, that's only fair.

Isaac is also up and gone, so let's count—Auguste, Tina, Isaac and the little one, that's three and one, you could make quarters out of that, in as many ways as there are quarters, crooked and straight ones, or from the top of the hat to the arms of the coats, or in any other way, or shiny, or smooth, or gruff, or never, that's the going thing, or that is the *gänger*, and the latter is also double, that's almost the norm now, something to be counted on, but can she count—Auguste, yes, Tina too, with Isaac it's a different story; but the little one will catch up easily, so far he has been frail, but we'll grant him that, and we'll also grant him the road, and also his milk bread, or at least half, for the road— because he will come through, he's a redeemer and he's a natural, not everyone succeeds like that, yes, no, no, we are surprised and dumbfounded, and he made it with nothing more then a piece of bread since the early morning, and nothing to drink either; but he didn't want anything, he had already accounted for himself, or counted himself out, yes, he can count indeed, in advance and also simple numbers, or both, or strict and en passant, and in secret, also openly, publicly, and he spends the love that is to come in advance, isn't he a gentle Croesus, four are better than one, he would say, if you asked him—learning it from the grave, pulling all the images and proceeding quickly, unawares.

Now pay attention, Isaac says, now it is enough, the girls follow, Auguste kills three tears with one blow, Tina cries and off they go, now we want to go down as much as up, the sun pushes us, the trick grows old, hurry now, let yourselves get lost, the ivy is poisoned, courageous daughters, the valuta is authentic, it has been freshly cleaned of all doubts, the eyes are still one with their gaze, focused, and clear is the weather, and the bouquet works. Nothing for us and nothing for you, and all that was immortal will lie behind us, this is how we leave it, right, how it gets branded into a smaller convoy, and how it gets drowned, and how it gets groped with all its edges, and this is how its hatches will be hardened, and how it will be left alone—and the levies will disappear, and the land will be scaffolded, and from now on when you say *left* it means *ahead*, and *right* will mean *the same*, at all times, whether you are heading seaward, or firmly landward, at teatime or at night—and so we leave things be and so we leave, and so this is where we are, and where was that, where is it now—and it keeps on spinning for a while in shallow waters, then it spins out, and roams about for the space of three abbreviations, and then you will give out a warning, putting to the test the tip-toes and the scalp, and then you frankly ask: Where is it, where was it, and then you let the questions dance, let them trumpet from the jungles, from the land-surveying office and from the Customs booth, and from the armchairs of your wretched idols—thus you ask, go on and ask, no one will guide you, no one else will unravel the direction from the twisted roads—Tina, scratch my back just one more time, but then we're off, and then you'll ask, then all of you will ask, you too my youngest, Hermann: not which, not who, not what, not why, not the purpose and not how much; then you will ask with your new voices this one thing, and I won't tell you what it is, just wade and see, through fields and far, and you won't know the question until it springs from your lips, until it is named, declared and written off: for never, for your featherless offspring, for all your absence, and for all your starved, skinny, roadless boldness—what's the name of the question? No, not Albany.

The Forgetfulness of St Ives

The forgetfulness of St Ives is vast, it floats up and down in unmistakeable oval patches of fog. These patches sink and rise yet they remain horizontal, no tilting has yet been observed. There are hints that the earth here has nearly remained a disc or at least indifferent to its own form, shapeless or otherwise. The forgetfulness of St Ives doesn't bother with injustices —people who drowned are also celebrated here, but not for long, and not all of them. The boy from L. is waiting in vain. His sister ventured out too far one day. And the day before she'd already put on a strikingly colourful dress. Let's be happy that we're all dressed in white and from St Ives. This is true. And his sister should have been happy, too. Will there be a celebration for her? Maybe not. She wasn't happy enough. But the boy from L. would like to wait a little while longer. Sometimes she was happy. For example, back when she waitressed at that big dinner party. She was also dressed in white back then. He saw it. And he also remembered it. But this is already a big indecency for

St Ives. Because forgetfulness belongs to St Ives the way tenderness belongs to other places—or fear, or hope, or reason. St Ives is as solitary with its forgetfulness as other places are with their hope.

Not much will come out of this forgetfulness. Large blackberries that everyone forgets to pick, though they are unforgettable blackberries, essentially tropical fruits of the north. Who will help the fish, or the sister of the boy from L. with her colourful dress? We don't need to help them, we need to help the world instead, let's be glad. In St Ives the world is welcomed and then forgotten, in the morning you wake surprised, and by noon you've forgotten all about it. The later you wake up, the faster you forget. Forgetfulness has developed its own economy here, but it's not a very complicated economy, all the drowned people see to that. And also the drowned fish, the seagulls and the kittens. And on a day when the severe southwester moves sideways over the land and threatens to tear apart the patches of fog, many unusual disputes occur: fuzzy vision, founding of sects, falls and fumbling hands—all the uncomfortable side effects of remembering. People in St Ives are not used to dealing with memory, and they don't want to get used to it. The small monument to forgetfulness at the curve of the road to the cemetery was created during a southwester that lasted for eleven days. It is an ambivalent object and people in St Ives would like to see it gone. The petitions to the city council are legion and some day they will probably show results. Yet those results are dependent on additional if only mild southwesters, otherwise the forgetfulness about the monument to forgetfulness will obstruct the decisions of the city council. This equality—as the forgetfulness is erroneously called in the better houses on the hills—is the real reason for the city council's tranquillity.

The boy from L. leans on the small monument, he is waiting for his sister. He rocks on his heels, whistling and rubbing his inflamed palms on the coarse stone he believes to be an erratic boulder. His sister did swim out too far. The dark plums of M.A. appear before his eyes, and once he has waited long enough, he will go to the bookstore and get them. He will take out his best suit. He will dine in fine clothes. The forgetfulness of St Ives is lost on him to a very small degree, and this degree is exactly what it deserves. It is this small degree of getting lost that we owe to forgetting. But what happens to those who are hungry? He can't leave this spot, unless he goes to the dark plums and his fine dinner. It's all his sister's fault. Perhaps they should have never left L., both of them. Their gloomy secret—L. That's what it was. That's what could have been, once. But it isn't. His wait, by now, is almost over, his hands ache slightly, but that was to be expected. That was how it was going to be. His vest is also coarsened by the stone. Also to be expected. And nobody knows who will win. All right, all right, you win, little sister. I won't wait any more. I will change my clothes, I will lean against a palm trunk wearing a white suit and photograph myself. Let's do it your way, even if it won't work. Then I'll eat and drink until nothing of the sky is visible any more. I can be a whole crowd, if I want to. Only me. I'm part of it, because I don't have to remember any more. I'm from St Ives.

This is what becomes of the boys from L. who end up here. Who all initially thought: *This can't be it*. But this is it. St Ives with its palm tree and forgetfulness, with the buoys that are never enough. The dark plums of M.A. will be good when their moment comes. And if I die I don't want to be troubled any more. More precisely: Once I'm gone, I want to be gone. Today the morning won't suffice any more—luckily the night has come. But one can never be quite sure. The grooved stones guarantee nothing. The dates are also grooved, the beautiful September and October dates which support and feed the night. The dates from St Ives. But no one else knows this.

The boy from L. leans out of the window now. Down below, the cars are swaying. And how they sway. There's nothing Mediterranean about them, this he knows. All memory is discarded. Sweet freedom. All the things that come to mind here. In L. this wouldn't have happened. Not in any other L. either, certainly not. For this to happen you would need a certain bridge, and a certain section of the path he used to walk with his sister. And you would also need Mr Peables with his pipe, who is not from here either. All the particular kinds of forgetfulness, all the way up to the particular forgetfulness which can't be classified. And here we have it. Always suspicious of maxims, of the trouble that comes with systemization. In such a way and in another way. And another, another, another. All the honeymooners who chose to come to St Ives don't know how right they were. Same goes for adolescent siblings. But maybe less so. Because siblings tend to know this a little bit more. In St Ives, the short excursion to the seal coves remains just what it is and where it is, it can't be dug out again, it won't get a second chance, and therefore it will never have been an excursion to the seal coves, because it is one. And certainly also because it is none. The difference begins to lose its significance, even if you can't hear it yet. It is a total loss. Anything that occurs in St Ives is long overdue. The freshly served sweet teas, and all the cookies. And the correct entries in church registers. And the short, black waves: Here is a wave which was never there. The stubborn barking. The stolen hats and shawls. St Ives has its own way of fighting against useless diversity, against all the shades of difference that span from one extreme to another. Starting with the goats on the hill up to, let's say—no, let's not say. Or the fishermen's wives? Nothing there, either. But we have beautiful waiters. We'll hire the boy from L. He's not suited for rescue operations or the like. He will turn out better than his colourful sister. He will pore only briefly over the morning papers in the evening. Over certain announcements, lists. He knows the bay is no guarantee for anything. He'll stick around.

Rahel's Clothes

What if I never again told the story about the ragmen in Kensington? Nor the one about Rahel's clothes in the closets, which weren't really closets but passageways to the other side of the street, or rather crawlways, although according to my calculations no one has been crawling through them any more, and not only because of Rahel's clothes? What if I no longer said anything, and answered questions only in the rarest of cases, and only to keep up appearances? *Do you happen to know why Rahel didn't take her clothes when she left?* Faced with such questions I could, if I was discreet enough, defend myself with long speeches. Speeches about the quality of Rahel's clothes, about closets as crawlways or crawlways as closets. And perhaps about the need for some good locks, and bolts, and additional safeguards. Until the person would breathlessly take his leave, protecting his hat against a sudden gust of wind, and without the slightest answer to his question, thinking: I'll never ask this person again. Another possible response to such a question would be to shake one's head, but that's already too talkative, and it could easily be perceived as a hint. The gesture would have a touch of secrecy, which discreet people avoid, and that's how you identify them, should you ever wish to identify them. Furthermore, this quick shake of the head would surely prompt the next question: *Or do you have any idea why Rahel hasn't asked for her things to be sent after her? After seventeen years?* To this question I could, if I hadn't managed to dodge it in the first place, without hesitation say no. Because I do not have an idea why this is so—I *know* why this so. And because you generally have no ideas about the things that you know for sure, and because you generally hunt down knowledge about things only in order to lose the ideas that you have about them, I would be absolutely right. Although once I did have an idea as to why Rahel didn't ask for her things to be sent after her, even though I already knew why. It was a dreadful idea. One of those dangerous exceptions to an old and useful rule, exceptions which are better avoided. And this was twelve years ago. Today, I no longer have an idea. I tell the truth. To which the other, hesitatingly, replies: *Seventeen years. If you stop to consider, that's a period in which a daughter could not only be born but also grow up.*

—Really, I could interject, stunned, for I wouldn't have thought to consider a thing like that. Such considerations belong somewhere with the ideas which the questioner, who *knows* nothing, still has. But if the conversation really took this turn, it would be better to quickly change the subject, because now I would be at risk of overwhelming the questioner with my knowledge and dispelling the rest of his ideas. Precisely at the moment when I believed my discretion to be unassailable, I would be at risk. At this point it would be better to bring the conversation around to daughters and sons in general, or even better to point out the bus which is possibly stopping at this very moment a few metres away and into which—after shaking hands hastily and mumbling a regretful remark—I lunge, only to ride dazed and exhausted into an unknown part of the city, while the other stays behind surprised and wondering what business I might possible have at this hour and on this bus, Number 147, for example. But at least Rahel's secret would be safe, and the shadow of her fate would have moved closer to my own—exactly as close as I came to denying my knowledge.

And on this occasion I could also—if I got off the bus at the third-to-last station and went to one of the small, south-west convent cemeteries—happen to find

Peggy's grave a few metres behind the rows of the venerable sisters, and with my English, which is better but not much better than my Spanish, I could translate the inscription on her grave as correctly or as falsely as I wanted. The only thing not in need of translation, since it's absolutely clear to me, would be the information written in numbers on the fading plaque— namely, that Peggy was born under the sign of Pisces and died at the age of seven, barely under the sign of Leo. And there would also be the years themselves which could prove to me—if I should, on this very afternoon, fail to have any idea that all our years are equally long gone—that Peggy's seven years are gone a little longer than the seven, thirty-five, or ninety years of many other people. Even those of her neighbour, whose name I'd probably forget and who at age fifteen, on a winter day, followed Peggy's fate, seemed in this manner of calculation to be less long gone than Peggy's years. And so forth. It must not have been a happy year for the convent, all these dying children, dying sisters, many from far away. I could try to imagine Peggy, how she walked down one of the long hallways and saw a window swaying in the wind, how she laughed out loud at the beginning of her dying. This I could imagine, this is as far as I could go. But only in the case of Number 147. There are other cases, and other numbers.

A taxi might also approach at the moment when our conversation about Rahel took a dangerous turn, and I could begin to shout and wave—again the hasty shaking of hands, the mumbled, regretful remark, and then the taxi driver's impatient question: Where to? How would I find the appropriate answer, lightning-quick and calm? Perhaps, in this very second, I would remember the street address of my half-Danish cousin, and perhaps I'd be lucky and she wouldn't be home, and once again I would catch the taxi, which was just about to make a U-turn, and this time give the driver, without even thinking and without knowing anything about Peggy, the address of the convent. I've never been there before, I would think, surprised, but only afterwards. And again I would land at Peggy's grave. But because my taxi would have been faster than the bus, I would now have more time to examine the inscription, and to consider the possibilities of transla-tion—so much time that I'd forget the time, until the advancing twilight would prompt me to leave the cemetery, and I would see the lights coming on in the various wings of the cloister, and cross the street, and skilfully slip through the garden gate, dodging a group of loudly talking former novices coming back from a reunion, and finally reach the gatekeeper's booth. And here, after asking the gatekeeper to call a taxi, and after her polite invitation to wait with her in the warm booth, for it is really quite windy, and after learning that nowadays there are no reunions of former novices (perhaps she would say *ex-novices*) but, rather, of sisters from around the world, and how they were *unfortunately* dressed in wildly different habits, I could bring up Peggy, in whose days the same habit was worn by sisters of the same order, a rule that was called into question as rarely as the daily prayer for a good death. *Surprisingly brave.* I could ask why it says *surprisingly brave* and thereby learn that the word doesn't mean *surprisingly* but *exceedingly, beyond all measure, in the highest degree.* My carelessness with foreign languages would have once again embarrassed me, but not too deeply, since the gatekeeper would now smilingly add that in any case you couldn't use the phrase *surprisingly brave* with regard to dying in this place, only *surprisingly fearful*, which in turn you couldn't put on a gravestone. And after a while, and a little more quietly, she would add: And it hardly ever occurs here, anyway. *Hardly ever, hardly ever*, the phrase would ring in my ears if I was lucky and the taxi pulled up this very second, thereby making sure that I did not learn anything further about Peggy, not that she was actually called Margaret, like many other Peggys, not that she came from Gloucestershire and not even that she came to this house at the age of four on the occasion of her father being transferred to a remote location in India. And therefore it would also not have occurred to me, on the way home, in the taxi, that the daily prayer for a good death must have become as natural to Peggy as the pattern of the stone tiles, bordering on a daily prayer for a *daily* death. And therefore, too, my ideas about Peggy would never be destroyed, instead they would be defined, precisely and eternally, by the phrase *hardly ever, hardly ever*, circumscribed and forever made inviolable, here in this taxi, on this very way home, and also in the equally certain and uncertain instant of my own final test. If one wants to call it that. I know many who want to call it that. But me? Do I want to call it that? Do I know myself? This question is unacceptable. Where have I ended up? The city lights are coming closer and clearer, there are the familiar neon signs, *Eliza Eliza*, the boutique at the corner where years ago I bought a hat, and there is also the proximity of our final stop, not yet fully recognizable to my eyes but already to my reasoning, however weak. Now quick,

quick, all my questions one more time. Who triggered them, who was it—Rahel, Peggy, the gatekeeper? Too late. Now there's no time left to look for stranger culprits. Now there are only the questions, and their chronology. How did it begin? With *the equally certain and uncertain location of my own final test. If one wants to call it that. I know many who want to call it that. But me?* Here. *But me?* This question is as dangerous as it is unavoidable. The question is not my fault. And I must go on: *Doesn't it remind me of the gestures of certain statues, frozen in the act of offering a blessing?* This question could possibly be avoided, but it's not very dangerous, and it's also exchangeable. The next: *Do I want to call it that?* This one might be a possible question but less hasty, not as blunt as before. What if I were more tender, if I asked the question more gently? Could I possibly arrive at my last question a little less unmindfully: *Do I know myself? Myself—myself—myself—myself?* This one reverberates, it is not right, it excludes almost nothing. I think I acted like someone who went forth to learn what fear was in order to not be afraid. I didn't heed the advice given, and with good reason, to those who wander in the dark, as they say (or so I believe): More fear, more fear, have enough fear, jump! *To wander*— even when I was seven this word made me laugh.

Again, one more time. My driver is slowing down, and the herb store where I buy my hollyhock tea is coming into sight from the other side. Quickly now. Quickly and gently, I still have it in my ear: *Certain and uncertain instant of my own final test. If one wants to call it that. I know many who want to call it that. But me? Doesn't it remind me of the gestures of certain statues, frozen in the act of offering a blessing? And do I want to call it that? Do I know myself?* Can you guess? Wrong guess, leave this question alone, it's lying. It's the one question that is not the one. It's the one that tries to trick me into cheap sleep. What is the name of the last question? Does it have a name, as we have names from the moment we enter the womb until very soon after, when our ashes float out over the abandoned vineyards and we no longer have a name? And all the time swearing that Solomon was not called Solomon, David not David? No—not *as we have names*, not so similar, not so false. This question must be even better. But how? What is the name of the last question? My driver turns on the overhead light and begins to read the meter, he will tell me the price any second now. *What is the name of the last question? What is its name?* Yes. That's the name. My car comes to a halt.

Cemetery in B.

We are still here. We can still be frightened by a small volte, and the necessity to summarize everything can complement our deaths. But to what end, when all the dead in the cemetery in Nancy have no idea about this, when they rest peacefully, too peacefully, as they were commanded to do. No summary then, maybe not yet. Decisions can be surprising. And that honey is called *le miel*, and that whoever knew the word would also say it, and then oversleep Orléans. For the sake of surprise, isn't that how it's said? So we'll stick with it, we won't be bedarkened, as little Kazimir Silhouette used to say, but no one understood him, not yet. And he was followed by a few Lord Osbornes, and *captains au long cours* in September, April and March. If we accept them as connections, as science does, we won't get very far. It's like heating up wine, and wine in these regions is useless when it's hot. Wine with honey—that was probably somewhere else. No need to understand this one. Never lose your fear completely. Always keep a small part of it. *Le miel* means honey, and people here stare at you when you buy certain things. No V for victory, there are rules in every country. That we know this. That we keep on driving. That we won't let these things intimidate us. What was accomplished was anyone's guess. It was too perfect. But you can take it with you. The way it's divided up so nicely, no one will notice. Okay, so let's go to the land's edge. Let's go to the *Privatcafé*. It was discovered by the Seventeen Somethings, although they never really count themselves. But they are always seventeen. One of us could lend you a little teakettle, just don't lose steam. And another could caress your legs with the golden moon. Then fate holds its breath for a moment. You know that. Everybody here knows that. But you should really visit little Kazimir, seven steps further up, he's long stopped growing, that helps. He plays chess with the captain, and the Lord Osbornes gather around and watch. 'Right,' they sometimes shout, 'right, Kazimir!' or 'Quite'. It depends. Enough now. You'd like to know what the chessboard is made of? Chestnut wood, I believe, but I don't believe it with certainty. I didn't look closely. Enough. You've been advised before you rush off with the borrowed teakettle and take the wrong turn. But then why? That's right. No one can deny your right to ask this. You are clearly undaunted. This helps to go on.

There is a glow spreading out from your barren table that you'll never understand. Be certain.

But that *le miel* is really called honey. That patience really goes so far. All the way from the amphorae to the steak houses. From the grand old names to the flat sea spray. Your Highness came to search for a ring. So far below? This is surprising, again. Will the ring bring luck? Does it have gemstones? So and so many karats, or higher? I am a king and I want to have my ring. Yes, this makes sense. But did Your Highness have breakfast? It's always easier to search for something when you've had breakfast, just my two cents. The heart must be calm. Strong and indifferent. Everyone knows this. Nevertheless it seems to be one of those commonplace truths that always go down the drain, and that, if you were at all serious, you needn't look up to, only bend down low. Anyone who has ever searched for a shoelace or a little rodent has this expertise. Or anyone searching for his conscience, when he stops to consider what the Black Prince did. What Pedro the Cruel did. Or something along those lines. Where did we leave off? Nowhere, Your Highness. We never leave. We always go back and forth.

Little Kazimir is much calmer. He sits in his own stony enclosure and plays chess with just about anyone.

Always the same game, continued with each new person. From time to time he smooths out his smock. And the Osbornes gathered quietly around, watching. The captain is sleeping. He's a good sleeper, one has to grant him that. He always was. On his big journey. It actually helped him. Bad sleepers are no use, not even mediocre ones. They have to be good sleepers, otherwise they'd go nuts. Otherwise the sea would dawn on them, and in general that's not very proper for a captain. The captain sometimes raises his head and asks 'Who's playing? Is it still little Kazimir, with whomever? And who's that standing around?' 'The Osbornes, sir.' That's it. The hour is resolved, certainly for him, if for no one else. Little Kazimir on his chessboard will keep in check anyone or anything that wants to encroach, or move towards other graves. He will probably keep them in check, and that's all he can do. The captain sleeps again. Sometimes he has a sore throat in his sleep, then he coughs and little Kazimir glances over at him quickly. But that doesn't happen often. The captain is not the same captain who always had a sore throat and therefore forgot how to capsize. He never learnt it in the first place. 'And this is good,' he says proudly, when someone asks. The Osbornes are silent. Little Kazimir nods politely but doesn't say anything either. His game frees him from the need to have opinions. And the Osbornes mostly want a game to be played, that's what they want the most. The changing players don't bother them. Sometimes they nervously put their fingertips together, but for other reasons. The king without a ring wasn't bad. He suggested a certain move on the chessboard and then he disappeared again. The move was a good one. Also the disappearing was pretty good. Perhaps the Osbornes consider this the art of kings. It takes a while to figure them out. Usually they have pointy faces, but there are also round faces among them. This needs to be said for the sake of justice. But not much more needs to be said for the sake of justice. People who do justice are easily embarrassed. You can't do justice to everyone. Or can you? People who know this will soon experience it. With the right amount of embarrassment, of course. Maybe one can. The captain sleeps. *Au long cours*, even in English—a long journey. The way this sounds. 'Normal,' says the captain in his sleep. He says it loudly. Three of the Osbornes smile. Little Kazimir looks up and instantly lowers his head again over his game. He hears hoofs clattering. It's probably Natalie. She stops, enters the church, and walks towards the quiet area to the right. She always makes a hesitant move on the board before she turns decisively and rides off. The Osbornes cough a little. Natalie's moves are not easy to deal with. Too much hesitation, and then too much decisiveness when the hesitation is over. The clattering of the hoofs is fading, but the chess moves remain. Can she do that? On her way out, Natalie never stops to correct her move, she thunders past. The sun goes down with lots of red, as if the sea were in need of correction marks. Kazimir makes another move. Natalie came from the lighthouse. Natalie always comes from the lighthouse when she thunders past. He understands that she's in a hurry. He is not, but she is. He understands that. He slips into his jacket. The Osbornes are getting restless. They misplaced their cardigans, perhaps on purpose. Only Philipp has one, Philipp Osborne. But what's one Osborne to do with a cardigan if all the other Osbornes are cold? They begin to walk up and down the short paths. The light goes on at Natalie's. She needs a vermouth. Kazimir hopes she'll get one. Maybe from the king, but you never know. Maybe not from the king. Kazimir can't give it to her. He is not a king, not an Osborne, he doesn't even have a sleeping captain who lies behind him on the left or on the right. What he has is an adventurous background: Jewish watchmakers, then many merchants, on both sides. But that's not the problem. Neither is the fact that he is too small. That he said farewell to growing, right after birth. He would find ways to reach the bottle and the glass. What keeps him is his game. Will someone else show up? He carefully adjusts the pieces and waits.

'We're already at the benches,' says the captain, leaning on his arms. 'At the benches,' repeats Kazimir. 'Take your hat,' says the captain. Kazimir ties his hat on. It's important to make sure that the captain is in a good mood. Perhaps he'll make another move. Or he'll go up to Natalie's and drink vermouth with her. 'Aye aye, sir,' says Kazimir quietly, and pulls on the straps of his hat. The captain taught him that. But the captain fell asleep again, he only needs his benches. The Osbornes also disappeared. To the front and then left around the second stone, as always. Their walks are as much a pretence as Philipp's cardigan. *Le miel* is honey. And Natalie stays alone. Where is Orléans? In Nancy? If only one of the Osbornes were here. Philipp perhaps. Yes, Philipp. Don't waste your thoughts. Kazimir memorizes all the positions, then he packs up his game and looks into the middle of the open stone enclosure. Into his short, deep grave. For the sake of surprise. This is how it's said. Kazimir knows this.

Wisconsin and Apple Rice

Should we begin to tell the old sentimental stories
once more? To summon pity? Which way are we trav-
elling exactly, Your Grace? Well, naturally we're going
this way. Downriver. Everything seems to depend on
us. Or does it? Oh, to let go, to let the questions be.
You admit there is a possibility that green will never
be green, you've already admitted it. And that the elves
have abandoned us. Well, let them. The fences keep
leaping into the frame, into the picture, you can clearly
see them. They quarrel with each other, and as they're
quarrelling, they start leaping around. But we stay here.
We wait. We wait to see what else the quarrel might
bring. Anything, really. Pictures. A story-telling lady
from California. Apple rice. Apple rice we both already
know, so they can't tempt us with that. The lady is very
good at telling stories. But it looks like she's bullying
her younger brothers. Let her. See, now we've become
suspicious again. Let her. She also talks too loud.
Let her, I said. Very well, the clip-on frame suits her.
Now she's coughing. She looks heavy. A heavy lady, and

talking. I'm telling you, it won't be enough. You'll see that it won't be. But for us it will have to be enough. Also, the apple rice. Whatever transpires, it shall always be enough for us. Ladies, black people in chains. Do you want to know what I think? We're haunted by what was denied. Everyone has been trying to teach us how to die with a smile. I see a cloister now in Wisconsin. They wash dishes there. Certainly very useful. They are kind to some people, over there. All this black-and-white. The lady from California wears a green blouse and a little black jacket. Right now I can only see her neck. But a moment ago she was wearing those clothes. Certainly. Though we should also get rid of certainly—of all the questions and all the certainties. But that's difficult to do. We have been well made, haven't we? How many are we anyway? Two? Are you certain? No, no, don't say anything, I already know. Everything is wrong. But only in its representation. The thing itself is right. The common thing. When the fences shift they make quite a clacking sound. And they are always shifting when they leap around. Now the lady is outside, Wisconsin is too, only apple rice is left in the frame. Apple rice is tireless. It hangs in there in such a way that it withstands all the leaping. It's very committed and it doesn't mind the quarrelling. It was probably prepared with love and without half a thought. All right, well, we'll have to make do with what presents itself. Although I'd have preferred a moon, half-full. Or a Greek letter —as a farewell sign. A letter from the middle. Because something smells like farewell. Like lead, like pencils. Which is appropriate for these circumstances. And it tastes like it, too. Believe me, this whole thing wasn't meant to be for the palate right from the start. The palate was supposed to be spared until nearly the end. But now we have lead on our tongue and apple rice before our eyes. There's the lady again. I didn't expect her to come back, really. She's tough. Do you think she ever stopped talking, outside the frame? I know, I know—no questions. Chief Littlewood didn't ask any questions either. Those aren't my words, *she* said that. It was meant as a joke, I believe, or supposed to be a joke. It's hard for the lady to get it right, having such a heavy face and all. I bet she's hiding a riding crop down where the frame ends. I find her touching. Which is a good thing. But she doesn't touch you. Do you think Wisconsin will also come back, the convent with the little dishwashing girls? No, better this way: Perhaps Wisconsin will also come back, the convent and all that. *Perhaps* should be allowed, I think. *Perhaps* must be permissible. *Perhaps* ought to be allowed to be called perhaps, otherwise nothing would be left. *Perhaps* should be protected by law. No one thinks of it. Most people don't like it. Nothing protects it. The lady up there has no use for *perhaps*. In her eyes, everything is what it is, and how it is. She shares this with her healers who are always giggling. But now she is alone. She can be kind of moving. But one mustn't put her upside down, on her dark crown, or she will fall over. And that would be that. How quickly everything moves towards us when it moves towards us. Leaping. You know this, too. It's a shame the pictures do not multiply. The lady. Wisconsin. Apple rice. Over and over again. Or perhaps it's not a shame. Or perhaps not a shame at all. We'll have to wait and see. It is possible that, in the end, only one of the three things will keep up with all the leaping. Or that they amalgamate. By now everything has come very close, don't you think? And we don't have much more room left behind us. At our backs, the drop-off is steep. Or it is not. Don't push me, I didn't pose a question. I only said: It's steep, or it is not. Luckily we're not alone. I mean, none of us are. Admit that we're lucky. But you won't admit anything. You're a listener, an eavesdropper, and only sometimes you resort to pushing. Now there's the clacking sound again. It sounds pretty mean. I think it's getting dangerous. If only the apple rice would disappear, the apple rice doesn't suit me. No reason, really. What are reasons? What reasons are. Should I say: I don't like the apple rice because it's ridiculous? I could say it. I mean, a splotch of rice could easily land in one's eye, if the stuff were real. But it does not look real. It hangs in there firmly. The apples too. Brown at the edges, but all the same. And Wisconsin seems to be pretty sturdy in its own way. The tiny convent. I don't worry about it. But if someone were to ask if we could ever get through the fences again, the small tin frames, by which I mean the empty ones of course, or even if we could get around them, I would say: No. By now, the only room that's left is behind us, one step. Or whatever you want to call it. Then there's nothing for a long time, and what comes after that is all foam. The foam will amalgamate us with Wisconsin, with the rice and the poor lady. We will be submerged into the freedom and choice we never had—wheezing, coughing and gurgling, but we're inside. I'd be curious to see you there, to see if you would dive towards the apple rice or towards the submerged convent kitchen? Will you be humming something when you wash up on the shore? You could hum the names of all the states. Or a shred of the stuff the lady told us, a shred.

But she isn't talking any more. She has fallen silent. That's a bad sign. And if it's not a bad sign, then it is a bad sign. The lady has left her mouth open, half open, which looks bizarre, she mustn't do that, tell her she mustn't do that, she must go on talking, tell her about Wisconsin and the apple rice for all I care, do you hear, tell her, tell her, pull her by the tangled strands of her hair, pinch her cheeks, but tell her: She must go on talking. She must go on talking.

II

Hemlin

Come down, Hemlin, guess what I have for you. Go down even lower. You'll never guess. Just don't vanish behind your humble figure, you don't need to do that, let it come to a stop. Let your figure come to a stop, I say, don't shuffle. One of your feet always lags behind. Do you understand me? No idea, but I think you are grumbling at the sun, you're becoming stubborn, that leads to nothing, that doesn't lead, right? Hemlin while you're at it, bring me a basket of soap! There he goes.

Hemlin, located in the state of Jackson, has a red-haired population, it never snows there. Hemlin can't be traced back to a duchy; it evolved with its citizens. Hemlin owes its open spirit to its mindful fishing industry. Hemlin will be the pride of its descendants. Hemlin has only a few short-term inhabitants.

Hemlin was sketched by Veronese. She stands facing the window, amidst her maids. She seems to be listening, trying to distinguish the sounds of the morning, and contemplating her own absence before she departs. Her right arm is angled, the hand slightly raised. The maids appear busy, almost fearful. Far behind them a door stands open. The maids, the door, Hemlin—nothing but the sketch is known. Veronese didn't execute the painting. Presumably he declined the commission after this sketch.

Hemlin is a letterhead. With an address, P.O.B., the usual thing, not a bad address. But not much effort put into it, either. The printing is unassuming, easy to miss on first sight. The predecessors had their heads stiffened by ocean wind, long before they came to this trade. Plain sailing, reliable. The pride of the young apprentices is visible. I come from Hemlin. They like to run errands. That's understandable.

Hemlin, a kind of unreasonable joy from causes which are in themselves reasonable. Well-known characteristic signs are found principally in the north-east, or more precisely the east coasts. Birdlike laughter, rapid growth, the joy of speaking through one's teeth and so forth. All this, described to the point of tedium even before Lawrence, has its origin in the human inclination to underestimate causes. These underestimated causes grow secretly, and then they break out. We'll spare ourselves a list of sources here.

Hemlin, Hemlin, where are you? Come on Hemlin, they will drown you, the sources are overflowing.

Hemlin must be a monument, round, makes trouble.

Hemlin.

Surrender

I hear the work is done with tricks and traps, with membranes, permeable stuff—bright, hellish bright. But *hell* can be many things. It's hard to get through. Whoever filled the corridors with milk was wise; this holds up, but only up to the ceiling. It does hold up. No more brain twisters. How much milk did Keats displace when he died in the millimetre-sized room? In the millimetre-sized room Keats died. The dull milk. The fading without which nothing will grow.

Without which the fields will fall disappear from the fables. No need to calculate the loss. The sky looks cloudy, it serenades the horses. Britannia's daughters blame the sky for nothing. Nothing. They were raised in the fresh open air, this always turns out well. It can turn out this way or that. Well, yes. There is no need for compassion where compassion is not needed. What does cricket have to do with worn-out saddle blankets, with letters from overseas communities?

Exactly. Here we lie, hares that we are. Unwanted, but still. We never cease to give up. Not a single little one of us, of our bright bunch. Bright is true. Though the camouflage colours were distributed unevenly. One could also say: We didn't take them, we proved incorruptible, we used our voicelessness, the tuning fork of the wise. The faults are obvious. *Intramuros*. Are there.

Since then they've been growing rampant, Gloucester, the vetches, I should like to catch a deep breath, sir, but certainly not for long. For long. *Vedo la cupola*, that's good enough. Not for you? I only ask. Because it's easily good enough for me. And wouldn't I like to know this, and wouldn't I like to have that. I would like to find the right measure. A rule. What does one follow? And yet I am. I draw a ruler, with light lines and with bold lines. There's also red in it.

A guiding light, nothing violent. Cobbler, stick—there he goes. From now on I will rely on the names only. On the names of hills, all kinds of names. I will try to act like someone who never arrives, someone untempted, someone untamed by silhouettes. Someone without trophies. I am still able to count until I am unable to count any more—five, six, too long. Way too long. The pact between us and us, do we want to give it its due? Undo it?

Salvage

Links, left, left, let. The lady sinks, the moulding crashes, other-wise it's nice and quiet. We all know the school of familiarity. There wasn't much to it, it was like that right from the start, easy. Her eyes are turned towards the sky, her eyes are colourful, even in the present uncertain situation. Hold the ropes, folks. Your lady's shoes are pretty. Barely worn.

Now things are about to turn upside down. Whatever is nestled in the corners will be pulled along. Cobwebs will be torn, hollow fences toppled—Attention in the front, don't dive as long as there's enough air, don't cough anything up that will come out by itself. To consider slogans as such, but who spoke of the after-maths? No word on that. Or was there? This pile of cardboard tubes is from the headquarters. Classified files. Floating.

The beds also topple and the darlings fly through the air, tattered themes, twisted laughter, white and wise— there it flies, and rolls back, wise enough to know the ins and outs, has known in and out too long, the reckoning is wrecked, the bill unsettled, all that added up now goes undone, and rummages, and longs for water, and it cannot be held by you, by anyone, folks—is there no straw man to clutch here? The old reckoning is weeping, is there really no straw man here? No one to remain, to rescue the reckoning?

Farewell, there might as well be grass growing here, *Ladies first*, I still have to see the doctor. General Lee had himself cast in wax, he or someone else, hadn't he? And he owned a pretty villa on the hill of shards. Make sure that the boys learn, adieu, adieu. That they grow— a waterproof solution. Cheap, I know. But nothing is the way it remains.

The happy day, one there was—it makes things sway, it makes others grind the water, then it stays away. Here and there the day set up cardboard mills without warranty—and here the water rises, all the names up to thirty-two, Lisbeth, Alfons, whitish, without a mark, and here the water rises unhindered, this was the condition, loyal mills, fulling mills, tinder mills, and stop—the day withdrew, it lets others do the grinding, it gathers in, *stands tiptoe*, it bows down and also sky-high, knows nothing but its mills—day, day, it doesn't know us any more.

Galy Sad

Jenkins complained about the shortage of vowels. Every week they are misplaced. The red river spit them out, that's old news. From before the ban. Jenkins? I think he confuses himself. He has no patience.

Jenkins stays away, he doesn't want vowels any more, he lies still, he's unreliable. I'll wait some more, but not for long. It's possible that he'll send a substitute. Be calm. No more new phrases.

Now he's put a pencil case over his head, expanded or not, and under it he's panting. But he doesn't take it off. That's how he is? Yes, just so. With the pencil case. The white coat doesn't fit, it's too long, and he's lying down all the time. Somebody should help him up. Few things work when you're lying down, very few things. Rivers are in no rush.

To fall. To wait, to wait, stop. Winnipeg wants to crochet another line around the ankles. Winnipeg is slow. She misspells herself and crochets straight lines, and always around. A line around our Jenkins' ankle, this she can do. Come down, Winnipeg, don't stay apart from us too long, do you want a horse? Yes, a horse. A little horse and crochet yarn. Will you come then? Crochet a sound for us, Winnipeg. And let your Jenkins sleep. His yearning for vowels will fade away, will splinter in the air, will soon cry its eyes out. A O U—go on, crochet, your Jenkins is sleeping, he is safe. He is resting. He remains lying down and visible, the way you left him, cast out, injured, slightly injured, go, go. And watch out for your crooked soles. Go away. He sleeps.

L. to Muzot

A small man with a mustard hat, that was Muzot. Don't bother me with your colours again, he cried. One is enough. Such talk always produces military men. Always? He shouted as much. It was so true. But Muzot was getting on my nerves. He had memories. I had to let him go. When I think of how he staggered out the front door—so small.

Litford stands at the front gate. He measures people. No one told him to, no one even gave permission. But he has authorization, he says. And a measuring tape. Or is it a ruler. No, he's ruled by his heart. You can't beat that. Sometimes he has chest pain and then I can quickly shoot past him. I've been measured three times already. I think I will tell him to continue with number four. Everyone here is already measured and the measuring tape ruins the tiles in my hallway. He's always taping. It's actually masking tape. I should tell him that.

L. wanted to go to Hampshire. But he didn't go, something stopped him. Perhaps it's the smoke around here, he said. But it doesn't help me if everyone's staying, I said. I don't like conversations that start this way. He notices. I couldn't be more clear.

Muzot said he has two sons, M. and M., but I don't believe him. He only wanted to intimidate me. Where did he get two sons? Perhaps he has two hats, M. and M. No, no, not even that. Sometimes I wonder where he might be now. M. and M.? That doesn't get us anywhere either.

Deep down in the shaft, L. hums when he passes my door. He has bad manners.

Mazarin visited me wearing his tunic. What do people want from me? He spoke of his thirteenth birthday. Me too. I am careful.

Litford measured L.—by mistake. But perhaps something came out of it anyway? A number, a result. Two hundred and eleven or a hundred and twenty to seventy. L. is tall. He has several sizes. I think this means trouble for Litford.

And trouble for me. We want to put him back on land, someone said. I heard him. Was it Litford? Not long ago he wanted to summon the management because of the pinwheel in the light shaft. And his measuring tape? No, I don't know if Mazarin left the house. This could have been arranged by Muzot. To put him back on land? I'd like to know where they get that land from. Everything is paved.

I know these things, they can't fool me. Lasalle doesn't stir any more either, I find that disappointing. I thought he wanted to come back. Because of the heavenly conditions here. For him at least.

Will I keep what's left? Will I hold it haphazardly to my heart?

Sur le bonheur

I read a piece about revolutionary architecture—I barely let it affect me. Should Versailles be expanded or not? For me this question is like a hole in the ground, a question of sequences. Expanded or not? Okay, okay. I don't give a feather about Versailles and it doesn't give a feather about me: I let it have its raven wings, I don't touch them, I admit that they grow. That they grow.

But yes: it was said to have been covered in black. But I don't see a thing. One mustn't take this too seriously, one must focus on the substances, all types. Or so I was told, so I conceded that it was said to me. Conceded several different things to myself. At that point I still hadn't come very far. Only as far as: like to, to the likes of—I still couldn't say anything, I couldn't protest. Everything was like now.

Where do they get the beautiful blackened stones? From stirrups perhaps. Now we need a Joker, one who passes through with his lights turned down. He should come. I'll let him decide in what way or manner— soundless would be best—but as he likes. I really won't grab him, he can count on that. I'll dodge him just in time.

Today I copied the rungs of ladders, one after another. I found out various things. A lotus between III and IV. The fourth turned out a little shaky. After that it went well for a while. Ladders, ladders, all kinds, but all the ladder work isn't perfect. Which is often the case. Who told me to stick to the rungs? I forget. W.V. or W.W., one of those. Should I stick to it? To my fourth, shaky rung? My favourite one? See what it can do?

The tower of Babel was certainly not built in a day. A cause for joy. There are many causes of this type. Everything is. Not in a day; certainly, certainly not, so many. Oh causes, these causes. I found your scarf. Do you hear me? I stopped climbing around the blackened beaches. I only found your scarf.

The valley, oh my valley, where I've always wanted to go. I never made it there, what a pity. Never made it to where I would have liked to begin, to begin oh so happily to flow. Would have. Where I would not have liked to stay. Happily, happily, but I never made it there. Never made it to where I wouldn't have stayed. Never made it.

Consensus

The words of confluence, hey, words, poultry, separated before the time that has yet to be defined: When should your sweet eclipses have struck, when did they get into each other's hair? No, no, I get it—gallantly and the sweat hardly tangible, resinous, which didn't even drop, nothing dropkicked, nothing drubbed beyond your soft assumptions, Alissa, the grave girl at the fire, and so forth—they meekly managed themselves out of this world, and sure enough their own initials, too.

The beauty of colourlessness, we'll hold on to it, and to youth, when no colour has yet been confirmed, that's it, that would be acceptable, youth. Who saw Thyrrus, saw the basket? Who saw whom, and whose heartbeat, the furs exchanged, the furs mixed up, who saw him? Him. Is Melbourne acceptable? Good, that was good, yes—this move will never be surpassed, Melbourne is already forgotten.

The darkness, then meandering paths, and finally the sequences—*pre-, main-, after-*, how is this so? *After-* is probably best, it is the very best, because it happened last, and in contrast to this the paths seem rather puny—smooth, no, not really smooth, but not ribbed either, even. Is it dark now? Not a trace. Meandering, but since the sequences have pushed themselves into the sequence of things, everything is swaying.

Ginger, Quadalupe or Kumawi? It sprawls, grows rampant all over our old traces, it keeps us in a sorry state, *the blue, blue Indian sea*, where to put it, well let's just leave it, the ground is still dry and it is still ground enough, it is dry enough ground, and why alone and why in front of fires, admit it, and let's get out of here, Kumawi, let's leave ourselves out of it.

Weary or not, who asks you a question, blind man? Alphonsus Liguori is far away, he lets the beaks float.

To preserve the proven immaturity.

Insurrection

The tracks of female jaguars, tendered in writing. I only hint. No signs of decomposition—those are reserved only for us. No, not in any other way. Reserved for us. Us, just like that. And that. Other people slurp fish oil. Let them. To choose between ten lyres and strum none of them. So. You were good.

You were very good, you were in control of yourself, in command, you had yourself. This already happened and didn't fail to happen, not a syllable. Given your sun. There was nothing to say.

Now give me back my willow trees. Smooth down your own fur, give me the willow trees. And take a rest, take a long rest. I will stay close to the edge. I want nothing of the current—except to be spared by it. The middle—gold, red-gold, black-gold. Spared until I'm no longer spared. Give me that.

Then the word flew up—senselessly into the turnip sky. No rabbit in sight, nothing snapped at it, not one hieroglyph was damaged. My animals don't like this kind of thing, they're not easily tempted. But the willow trees must be here, the shrubs, even the trunks. How is this supposed to work? These are none of my questions. Left, right, there's people, craftsmen or something, pretty and strong enough. Z.V.B. and not to be underestimated.

The old formulas have expired, none repeat.

Quiet now.

Queens

Kindred spirits, finally accomplished, the viruses of vertigo stringing themselves together, *uses my wife for sewing*, the chainmail shirt grows, soon it can be hooked on, the legend itself an instruction for reading, a sewing thread for the immortals, for their fragile fingers—slipping away—unthread the needle, no, no, not like that, in a minute we'll find each other again, we are complete, here, yes, here, we're screwed up in Virginia but we're still here.

Read, read, the low shrubs, what kind what colour, in the wording of what halves, river valleys, *layouts*, is it so easily said, isn't the rivulet rising, read, read further, the rust, the scrawny lines, curled, the flipped pages and the lines, read and listen, don't stand by yourself, three sixty-eight is a good number, it won't stay, go ahead and take it.

Uses my wife, the sewing table is good, with plenty of screws, it holds up well and lets itself be, it's also written into the plan and it doesn't give up, standing there and there, containing its own end and all measured, all sewn up, not good enough but good, it rattles, funny is a word for whoever lets it be. And hay is another, it doesn't fit, it's wrongly cut. Hay, who said it? No one, no one said hay. Or someone who doesn't admit it. Hay is a word.

Fare well now, Mary, farewell, it was nice to serve you, you have passed. Here are the two flat steps—watch out—now it goes down but only a little, only slightly down, just like you wanted it and not for long, the carnations are waiting, don't fall, forgive whatever you find here, leave the shirts in the garbage, *don't look back*, again—this is getting too familiar, *back, back*, the view is good, as is the advice, so don't look, don't listen, Mary, go.

This isn't supposed to be an ending if it's supposed to be one, there are enough ends, lengthwise and lengthwise, at your feet and at your feet, if you want— endlings, fourteen snippets, *synthetics*, pearls and the devil, this works, Mary—everyone believes it, how it all swoops down from the table, so let the ends dance until they are rounded edges and ends rounded with ringlets, until they're gathered, our good friends, into the soaked book on which we swear.

CODA

Snow

Snow is a word and so is hay. Snow is a word. There are not many words. There are not many that don't name what they are one with because they don't name it. Or that are not one with what they don't name because they are one with it. Yet snow is a word. Whether it fails to fall, starts to fall slowly or swirls down in gusts, it can't fight back. It is a word. In the fists of children, on the roofs, on the crests of mountain creeks with which it quickly fuses—wherever it is, it is a word. Snow! the children shout, and sometimes they also shout: The snow! Which is not accurate. Which leads to *my snow, your snow, our snow,* to all the possessive inaccuracies which stop one from wanting to open one's mouth altogether. It also leads to *no snow.* Then the long summer returns. Luckily we have hay, for hay is also a word. And many words there are not. But let's stick to snow. Recently a chamberlain who knew I'm always searching for words told me what a chamberlain is, and I nodded as if I understood, because I didn't. All I understood was that it is not a word. Which is a lot, and we would have parted peace-fully had not the chamberlain all of a sudden exulted: *The beautiful besnowed schoolhouse!* This made me so furious that I turned on my heel and ran away. When I came to my senses an hour later and turned on my heel again to look for him, he was gone. He was gone, just like the village and his schoolhouse encased in snow. Nothing was besnowed any more. There are bespeckled trout and begrimed poodles, but already with the poodles I'm not sure if one shouldn't better say poodles encased in grime. *Be, be*, this saggy *be*-which has little to do with the woes of a poodle and even less with the falling of, the lying still of snow. A village can be encased in snow and so can a school-house, but for me nothing can be besnowed.

En–, the first syllable of English, goes back to Middle English and Old French, so when there is the sense of 'to cause (a person or thing) to be in something' (*The Prefix En- and Its History*, Boston, 1907)—how should it therefore not belong to snow and snowing a thou-sand times more than any other prefix? Whoever searches for snow in various etymologies will find it, depending on the nature of his search, after infestation

…10). The translators express their gratitude to the …blishers.

The texts 'Memories for Samuel Greenberg'. …urrender', 'Salvage', 'Galy Sad', 'Queens' and 'Insur-…ection' appeared in *Lana Turner* 10.

The translators wish to thank the Austrian Cultural …Forum New York which generously supported an ear-…lier stage of this translation with the Austrian Cultural Forum Translation Prize in 2009, as well as the National Endowments of the Arts for a Translation Fellowship in 2012.

The translators also thank Isabel Fargo Cole for her incomparable translation advice, and Ilse Pam Dick for reading an early version of the manuscript.

and secondary school, and before vanilla and view, before wall and weapon, after horizon and humanity.

These are our choices, things we can compare. One can also rightly maintain that rain comes before snow in more than one respect, but I've been suspicious of everything that one can maintain rightly for a long time. One can either maintain something or not. If one can not maintain something one quickly assumes that one can maintain it rightly. And since of the many things that are maintained one can mostly not maintain anything, this phrase is on the rise. Maintaining comes before raining in this very odd order we've surrendered to. It also has more to do with raining than rain does with snow. And I don't maintain that rightly. Maintaining and raining usually go too far but in most cases don't achieve what matters. If at the time of the Flood it had snowed and not rained, Noah's selfish ark wouldn't have helped him one bit. And that's only one example.

Translators' Acknowledgements

The texts in the first section 'My Lang[
taken from the collection *Eliza, El[
published by S. Fischer Verlag in 1965)[
republished as part of the *Gesammelte Wer[
Works]* in 1991, it also included the st[
Sprache und ich' (My Language and [
Schwestern Jouet' (The Jouet Sisters) whic[
later in 1968. For this volume the texts [
arranged chronologically according to th[
composition. The publishers and translator[
their gratitude to S. Fischer Verlag for permi[
translation and publication of these texts.

The section 'Bad Words' represents the enti[
Schlechte Wörter as it was first published by S. F[
Verlag in 1976.

A short text entitled 'Schnee' (Snow) was c[
posed in 1975 but not published until the 1987 col[
tion of autobiographical prose and notes *Kleist, M[
Fasane*.

Earlier versions of the texts 'Bad Words' an[
'Hemlin', along with a shorter version of the introduction, appeared in *Poetry Project Newsletter* (March–April

and secondary school, and before vanilla and view, before wall and weapon, after horizon and humanity.

These are our choices, things we can compare. One can also rightly maintain that rain comes before snow in more than one respect, but I've been suspicious of everything that one can maintain rightly for a long time. One can either maintain something or not. If one can not maintain something one quickly assumes that one can maintain it rightly. And since of the many things that are maintained one can mostly not maintain anything, this phrase is on the rise. Maintaining comes before raining in this very odd order we've surrendered to. It also has more to do with raining than rain does with snow. And I don't maintain that rightly. Maintaining and raining usually go too far but in most cases don't achieve what matters. If at the time of the Flood it had snowed and not rained, Noah's selfish ark wouldn't have helped him one bit. And that's only one example.

Translators' Acknowledgements

The texts in the first section 'My Language and I' are taken from the collection *Eliza, Eliza* (originally published by S. Fischer Verlag in 1965). When it was republished as part of the *Gesammelte Werke* [Collected Works] in 1991, it also included the stories 'Meine Sprache und ich' (My Language and I) and 'Die Schwestern Jouet' (The Jouet Sisters) which appeared later in 1968. For this volume the texts have been arranged chronologically according to the date of composition. The publishers and translators express their gratitude to S. Fischer Verlag for permitting the translation and publication of these texts.

The section 'Bad Words' represents the entirety of *Schlechte Wörter* as it was first published by S. Fischer Verlag in 1976.

A short text entitled 'Schnee' (Snow) was composed in 1975 but not published until the 1987 collection of autobiographical prose and notes *Kleist, Moos, Fasane*.

Earlier versions of the texts 'Bad Words' and 'Hemlin', along with a shorter version of the introduction, appeared in *Poetry Project Newsletter* (March–April

2010). The translators express their gratitude to the publishers.

The texts 'Memories for Samuel Greenberg'. 'Surrender', 'Salvage', 'Galy Sad', 'Queens' and 'Insurrection' appeared in *Lana Turner* 10.

The translators wish to thank the Austrian Cultural Forum New York which generously supported an earlier stage of this translation with the Austrian Cultural Forum Translation Prize in 2009, as well as the National Endowments of the Arts for a Translation Fellowship in 2012.

The translators also thank Isabel Fargo Cole for her incomparable translation advice, and Ilse Pam Dick for reading an early version of the manuscript.